Ex-CIA agent John Harrison, his Israeli girl friend Zahava and Greg Farnesworth of the Leurre Oceanographic Institute were exploring an ancient temple when, suddenly, a high-pitched, whining noise filled their ears . . .

When they came to, they found themselves inside a spaceship driven by K'Ronarins, whose ancestors had built the underground matter transporter thousands of years ago.

Their destination: Earth. But a subtly different Earth than the one they had known. A planet that had already been invaded by a force dedicated to wiping out all human life in the galaxy!

STEPHEN AMES BERRY

THE BIOFAB WAR

ACE SCIENCE FICTION BOOKS
NEW YORK

THE BIOFAB WAR

An Ace Science Fiction Book/published by arrangement
with the author

PRINTING HISTORY
Ace Original/May 1984

ISBN: 0-441-06226-1

Ace Science Fiction Books are published by
The Berkley Publishing Group,
200 Madison Avenue, New York, New York 10016.
PRINTED IN THE UNITED STATES OF AMERICA

To my wife, Linda, and our small Zahava, with love.

I'm indebted to my friend Crazy the Spy for much that went into Sutherland and Bakunin. And I'm very fortunate to have so fine an editor as Beth Meacham.

Thanks to Janice Kaidan for all that typing— blessings on her band.

No storm is so insidious as a perfect calm, and no enemy is so dangerous as the absence of enemies.

—**Saint Ignatius Loyola**

Man-in-seed, in seed at zero,
From the star-flanked fields of space,
Thunders on the foreign town
With a sand-bagged garrison . . .

—**Dylan Thomas**
"The seed-at-zero"

THE BIOFAB WAR

CHAPTER ONE

"Mr. N'Trol," said Captain J'Quel D'Trelna, "how much longer on the shield, please?"

"Watchend, Captain," replied *Implacable*'s Engineer, his distraction clear over the commnet. "We'll have it up by watchend."

"You've been telling me that for the last three watches, N'Trol."

"We've gotten the security shielding on line, Captain. The two systems shouldn't be interdependent, but they are. Someone must have run out of parts just before the Fall, so they jury-rigged repairs, and that's the way she went into stasis. Only now can we concentrate on the external system."

"Thank you, Engineer," said D'Trelna sardonically, "for the insight into Imperial ingenuity. But I'm not concerned with security shielding. There's not much chance we'll have a S'Cotur assault force to localize this far from home. Will you guarantee me external shielding by watchend?"

"No, sir, I will not. And Captain, if you wouldn't keep asking me for a progress report every time I pick up a spanner, the shield might be up now. Of course, if you'd care to come down from the bridge and lend a hand . . ."

D'Trelna switched off with a snort. Swiveling the command chair back toward the big screen, he caught sight of H'Nar L'Wrona's grin. "Something funny, Commander My-Lord-Captain?" he asked, exaggerating the title.

"You can't bait me with that anymore, merchant," the XO said good-naturedly, turning back to his console. "And you

1

really shouldn't harass N'Trol. He's the best engineer in Fleet—probably the only one who could have kept this relic moving across the galaxy.''

D'Trelna sighed. "I know. But we'll be coming out of hyperspace soon and I feel naked without a shield.''

L'Wrona bent toward a telltale, hiding his amusement at the sudden vision of D'Trelna naked. Half again the slim aristocrat's age and three times his size, the Captain's image would never adorn a recruiting poster. Luckily for them all, the ex-S'Htarian trader was as brilliant as he was large.

L'Wrona looked up. "Be logical, J'Quel. We're a long way from the war. There's no reason for the S'Cotar to be this far out. Probably no reason for us to be, either.''

"L'Guan called this a vital mission, H'Nar,'' said D'Trelna, invoking Fleet's Grand Admiral. "If Archives thinks there's a chance of finding an intact Imperial matter transporter anywhere in this galaxy, then a ship must be sent. Look on it as a shakedown cruise.''

"Maybe.'' L'Wrona shrugged. "But how many missions sent at Archives' request have turned up anything? Two? Four? Out of how many? A hundred?''

"Yes, but one of those was an Imperial citadel with a flotilla of cruisers in stasis.''

"A badly functioning stasis field, J'Quel. And at least one still badly functioning ship. Our communications, our weapons, and our defenses are unreliable.''

"No need to remind me.'' D'Trelna dialed up a cup of steaming hot t'ata from the chair arm. "At least the beverager works.'' A chime sounded.

"Coming up on space normal, gentlemen,'' said K'Raoda, the very young, very bright Subcommander manning Navigation. If they get any younger, thought the Captain, suppressing an urge to check with N'Trol, we'll have to toilet train.

"Very well, Mr. K'Raoda.''

"Shipwide,'' he said over the commnet. "This is the Captain.'' His voice echoed through the long miles of *Implacable*. "We're about to enter a star system unexplored since the Fall. As we're far from home and the S'Cotar, I expect no trouble. Just to be safe, though, we'll be going to battlestations. All personnel will don warsuits. Captain out.''

Accepting the silvery packet from a yeoman, D'Trelna rose, unbuckling his long-barreled blaster and setting it aside. Shaking open the warsuit, he tugged it on over boots and brown duty uniform as did the rest of the bridge crew.

It didn't look like much, that bit of silver foil. A recently recovered product of the millennia-dead Empire, its secret still a mystery, the warsuit could briefly absorb ion fire and doubled as vacuum and pressure suit.

Feeling slightly foolish in the safety of the great old ship's big bridge, D'Trelna twisted on the transparent bubblehelm. Snapping his blaster on, he sat back down. "Let's do it, Commander L'Wrona," he ordered.

"Battlestations. Battlestations," L'Wrona intoned, the klaxon briefly seconding him.

"All sections report ready," said L'Sura from the Tactics station.

"Stand by for space normal," K'Raoda said. All eyes turned to the big screen, now showing only the gray of hyperspace.

"Space normal . . . now!"

A tugging at the stomach, slight pain in the head, and it was over. Swirling nebulae and a billion hard points of light filled the screen, set among the obsidian of space normal.

"So. Here we are," said D'Trelna. "Anything, H'Nar?"

The XO's long, tapering fingers flew over his board. "Nothing," he said finally, looking up from the telltales. "At least nothing hostile. Primitive radio signals from insystem somewhere. Too fragmented for immediate analysis. I'll put computer on it. Alright to launch a homing probe?" At D'Trelna's nod, he gave computer the order.

What looked like one of the many small hull instrument pods detached itself from the cruiser. Following the transmission traces, it shot away toward the small sun.

"What have you for me, Mr. K'Raoda?" asked the Captain.

"Class five sun, seven to ten planets—I'll firm that up soon. No ships' traces. No functioning Imperial commbeacons or navbeacons."

Trying to scratch his balding head, D'Trelna's hand met the helmet. Grunting, he twisted it off, setting it in his lap.

"Which means we'll have to probe from planet to planet, looking for Imperial remains."

"Best chances are with the inner planets, given this system's configuration and those signals," said L'Wrona.

"Agreed." The Captain nodded. "Follow that probe, Mr. K'Raoda.

"H'Nar," he said, rising, "have them stand down to alert condition. I'm going to get some sleep. Call me if anything, anything at all, happens.

"You have the conn, Commander," he added formally, relinquishing his chair and his ship to L'Wrona and heading for the closed armored doors. "And check on N'Trol."

Leaning back from the deskscreen, D'Trelna reread the diary entry:

Arrived today in star system unexplored since Imperial dreadnoughts kept the Pax Galactica a very long time ago. I'm beginning to believe this is yet another stupidity conceived by the morons in Archives and implemented by the cretins of Intelligence. Have detected no Imperial traces. Have detected possible primitive civilization farther insystem. Have launched and am following survey probe.

Ship in need of sundry repairs—hasty nature of refit becoming painfully obvious. Main shield has been down for eight watches, two fusion batteries couldn't heat a cup of t'ata and our antiship missiles have twice homed in on Recreation Deck's lavatory.

Only really dangerous problem is shield. If we met a S'Cotar task force now that did not obligingly teleport into a security shielded zone, such as Hangar Deck, they'd have us for dinner.

Ever-sensitive to his weight, he changed "for dinner" to "by the shorts."

Filing the diary back into computer, D'Trelna punched up and devoured two large helpings of calorie-laden o'rna, then

dropped into bed, hands clasped contentedly over the swell of
his belly, blaster tucked under his pillow.

Awakening at midwatch, he called Engineering. "Well?"

"Fine, thank you, sir. And yourself?"

"N'Trol, no one likes a smart mouth. Shield status,
please."

"Still down, but . . ." He continued hastily, forestalling an
awesome tantrum, "we've traced the flaw. A relay behind
some Hangar Deck bulkheads. I've got two techs on it. Should
have heard from them by now."

"Check and advise. Bridge. H'Nar? Noble Captain here.
Where are we?"

L'Wrona switched the screen to plot. The red dot of
Implacable was projected between the fifth and fourth green
orbs from the big yellow disk occupying screen center. "Halfway between the fifth and fourth planets, J'Quel. The smaller
planets are insystem. We've confirmed radio signals coming
from number three. Otherwise, sensor probes negative. The
outer worlds we've passed so far would probably not have
attracted the Imperials—unfit for habitation. Number three's
our best chance." He glanced at his board. "Coming up on
number four now. Several small moons. Little atmosphere.
Just another dead—" He broke off, blinking.

"K'Raoda, L'Sura, check radiation sensors. Mine just
swept off scale." He ran it back. "N seventeen."

"Confirmed."

"Confirmed."

Computer broke in with an asexual urgency. "Alert! Alert!
N seventeen. N seventeen. Request battlestations. Request battlestations."

"Captain, an N seventeen sweep," L'Wrona said tersely.

"Peak, down, off?" D'Trelna rolled out of bed.

"Yes. That could only be—"

"I know what it is," he said, pulling the warsuit on over his
rumpled underwear.

"But this far out?"

Another voice came into the commband. "Bridge. Engineering officer. I'm unable to raise anyone on Hangar Deck."

"Captain here. Stand by, N'Trol.

"That's it, H'Nar. Hangar Deck. It's their standard assault pattern—vector on the largest open part of a ship." He tugged on his boots. "Apologies to you, N'Trol. Thank fate you got security shielding on line.

"Very well, H'Nar. Speed, not subtlety." He stood, holstering on the blaster. "Shield and seal Hangar Deck. Battlestations. I'm closer; I will command the counterattack. You trace that N seventeen to their base and take it out."

"J'Quel," the XO protested, "you're too old for a firefight. That's my duty."

"I am not too old, I am too heavy. But there's no time to change places. If nothing else, I'll draw fire from the assault. Out." With that, he ran into the corridor, covering the ten paces to the nearest lift as the battle klaxon rattled off the walls, sending bleary-eyed officers running for their posts.

Sealed behind the bridge's thick battlesteel, L'Wrona sat in the Captain's chair, softly drumming his fingers on the arm. "Well?" he demanded, unknowingly mimicking D'Trelna.

K'Raoda looked up, shaking his head. "I need another transmission for a fix. It could be either the planet or one of its satellites."

"Bridge, Engineering," came N'Trol's unmistakable gravel voice. "We've bypassed that faulty relay. I can give you seventy-five percent external shield now."

L'Wrona shook his head, eyes still on the screen with its tactical scan of nearby space. "Negative, Engineer. Leave the shield down. And drop Hangar Deck's security shield. Be prepared to raise both instantly on my order."

The challenge came at once. "Flanking Councillor two to Imperial seven."

"Arcon five to Flanking Councillor seven." Nonsensical as an i'worr move, it made a good authenticator.

"Very well, sir. We'll await your order."

K'Raoda looked up from the half-finished trace pattern threading across a telltale. "What are you doing, sir, if I may ask?"

"Getting you your N seventeen, Subcommander. They know we're at battlestations. But we haven't moved on Hangar

Deck yet, and I've dropped security shielding, so they may well think it a drill. I'm hoping they'll take the opportunity to flit reinforcements aboard before moving deeper into the ship. When they do, complete your trace."

"But we're at battlestations," protested L'Sura. "They'll think primary shielding is up."

"Don't worry," L'Wrona said, "I'm about to tell them it isn't." Before he could do anything, the commnet chimed.

"H'Nar, we're in position. Have you gotten a trace yet?" At the head of fifty commandos, the Captain was pressed against the gray wall of corridor A-10. Around the next curve, the double access doors to Hangar Deck were sealed shut.

"No, sir. I was about to inspire it."

"Inspire it, then. Let's get this over with. Computer. Captain. Leave this channel tied into Commander L'Wrona's and acknowledge."

The machine beeped its response.

"XO to Hangar Deck," L'Wrona said languidly.

"Hangar Watch. Ensign U'Rola," replied a familiar, cheery voice. A dead man's voice.

"XO here. Shield's still inoperative. Engineering wants a two-man maintenance shuttle readied. Seems we've a faulty hull repeater."

"Very good, sir. It'll be ready when they arrive."

"Thank you, Mr. U'Rola. Bridge out.

"Did you get that, J'Quel?"

"Good, aren't they?" said the Captain coldly, checking his bluster. "We'll see just how good in a moment."

"N seventeen." K'Raoda adjusted a setting. "Got the little slime. Mark seven, one four nine three. The nearer satellite."

"Well done." L'Wrona nodded. "Mr. N'Trol, both shields now, please. Mr. L'Sura, flank speed for target. Stand by gunnery.

"They're all yours, merchant."

Peering cautiously around the corner, D'Trelna saw the security shield's hazy overlay blurring the doors. "Computer," he said, striding purposefully toward the doors, weapon leveled, "this is the Captain." Behind him the commandos fell into skirmish order, long, lethal M-32s at highport. "On my command, you will override the seal on Hangar Deck access A-ten and breach security shield to admit my party and me. After we enter you will seal and shield the access, opening only on my or the Executive Officer's direct, confirmed order. Acknowledge and confirm.''

"Acknowledged. Assault Leader four to Admiral's phalanx nine."

"Imperiad four to Admiral two."

"Order confirmed."

D'Trelna looked at D'Nir. The young commando Sergeant nodded. "Computer. Open access doors A-ten and breach shield."

Before the doors were halfway back, D'Trelna charged through, an angry bull heading straight down the center of the cavernous hangar. The familiar sight of shuttles, scouts, and fighters nestled in their soft-lit berths did not reassure him. Something was wrong: it was too quiet. Hangar Deck was never quiet. There should have been sixty crew on watch, performing the necessary drudgery of maintenance and security. Nothing moved. Only the soft padding of the troopers' boots broke the uncanny silence.

Not pausing, not turning, D'Trelna waved his weapon to the right. A squad broke off, running for the ramp to Hangar Control, recessed behind a great slab of one-way armor glass high above the gray deck.

Walking from behind a shuttle, duty log in hand, a cherub-faced ensign looked up, astonished at the sight of the advancing commandos. "Captain?" he asked, smiling uncertainly. "Why the invasion?"

As he stepped toward U'Rola, D'Trelna's communicator screeched. Unhesitating, the Captain fired a bolt straight into the Ensign's chest. His form rippling, U'Rola dissolved into a dark-green insectoid. It fell to the deck, a hole seared through its thorax. Bulbous eyes staring sightlessly at the distant ceiling, it lay with legs and tentacles twitching as the humans stormed past.

From atop the flat-roofed shuttles and from behind landing struts, the distinctive indigo of S'Cotar blaster fire lashed out. "Assault!" D'Trelna shouted needlessly, snapping off a shot as his warsuit took a bolt. The commandos swept past him, closing with the shapes that flickered in among the shadows, angry red lightning blasting from their rifles. As they zig-zagged in among the craft, blue ion fire touched but did not harm them, deflected by the warsuit's ancient magic.

Unprotected by resurrected Imperial technology, the S'Cotar warriors fell back into an ever-tighter circle until, cornered before the great hangar doors, a final volley finished them. D'Trelna personally killed their last transmute, distinguishable from its warriors by a thinner exoskeleton and tapering upper tentacles.

"L'Wrona," coughed the Captain, gagging on the stench of burnt bug, his bubblehelm prematurely removed, "I'm happy to report that the warsuits work. Saved my life about a dozen times."

"We've wiped out their assault force—and without taking any casualties. They got the hangar crew, of course. Must have flicked the bodies into space. Have you hit their base?"

"We have." The XO stared at the blasted ruins mirrored in the screen. "They stopped the first missile wave, but the next took out their shipbusters and the third finished them. Medium-sized surface base; not hardened. Punched through their shield with the first fusion salvo. We avoided most counterfire, but I'd hate to shoot it out with another cruiser without max shield."

"Very well, H'Nar. I'm coming up." Turning, he headed for the corridor and the lift. "Tidy up, Sergeant D'Nir," he ordered, glancing at the S'Cotar corpses now being stripped of weapons and heaped middeck for disposal. The viscous green ooze that was their lifeblood spread slowly from the pile of bodies.

Stepping into the lift, D'Trelna sketched his action report: the alarm had been quickly sounded, the area sealed, and the ship's reaction force, under his personal command, had killed the S'Cotar and wiped out their small base. The enemy vanquished, *Implacable* continued her mission. And yet . . .

There were some disturbing issues raised by the attack. The Captain voiced one as he sank wearily into the command chair, dialing up a fruit drink. "What are the S'Cotar doing this far out on the galactic arm, H'Nar?"

"Perhaps they're also looking for Imperial gear." Thoughtfully, he tapped the tip of the laser stylus against his teeth. "Question is, how long have they been out here? And why?

"Also, J'Quel, while we've been fighting, the probe's been busy." He nodded toward Survey, where K'Raoda now sat, intently reading a telltale. "Those radio transmissions are confirmed. Early cybernetic-age civilization on the third planet."

"Cousins?" asked the Captain, knowing the answer.

"As usual, according to preliminaries. The Empire must have seeded half the galaxy."

"Why haven't the S'Cotar enslaved or exterminated those people, as always?" D'Trelna crumbled the empty cup between thick, blunt fingers, tapping it into the chair disposer. "The force we just beat could easily have taken one backward planet."

"Well, only one way to find out," said the XO. "If this system holds any help or any answers, that world is the place to begin."

"Agreed.

"Mr. K'Raoda," he said, swiveling toward Survey, "if you can break away from those readouts for a moment, I will take damage control and casualty readouts at my station.

"Mr. L'Sura, resume original heading for planet three.

"H'Nar, please stand down from battlestations. Maintain high alert."

Triumphant from her first battle in five thousand years, *Implacable* left the molten ruins of Demos and headed in toward Terra.

CHAPTER 2

LOOKING UP AT the small TV, John Harrison groaned. Sutherland! Not now! Why couldn't he ever call? This was carrying professional paranoia too damn far.

Impatient, the casually dressed, middle aged man rang the doorbell again.

"Coming, Mother," John called over the intercom. Sutherland responded with a thumb ambiguously raised to the camera.

Padding barefoot along his townhouse's carpeted hallway, Harrison opened the door, letting in Sutherland and the smell of blooming lilac. Down the block, the first produce stands of the day were setting up in front of Capitol Hill's Eastern Market. It was only eight, but already the air was moist, the sun too hot for April. It was going to be an early spring scorcher.

"Don't you ever sleep?" asked John, leading the way back to his office.

"I've had myself cloned."

"You look like hell," added the CIA's Deputy Director for Special Operations, taking in the bleary eyes, rumpled shorts, dirty T-shirt and two days' worth of beard. "The eternal dissertation?" he asked, stepping into the sunny office.

"No." They sat, John at his desk, Sutherland on the white Haitian cotton sofa next to the fireplace. "*Certain Aspects of the Interrelationship of Cartesian Dualism and Quantum Mechanics* is finished.

"Coffee, Bill?"

"Please."

John poured from the grimy glass pot, handing Sutherland a white-and-blue mug. The CIA officer glanced at the caduceus etched into the front. "You on the KGB's Christmas list, John?" he asked, sipping cautiously.

"Christ, I hope not. No, that's from a little gift shop in McLean, William. It's run by an elderly DAR matron. A couple of your guys told her they were physicians at Georgetown and got her to special order a raft of these." He hoisted his own mug. "If she ever finds out the truth, it'll kill her." They chuckled evilly.

"So, the thesis is finished?"

"Yeah. And I think I survived my orals. We'll know next week."

"So why the midnight oil?"

John sighed. "My book. My unfinished book for which I unwisely accepted an advance." He swept his mug over the desk top litter: canary legal pads covered in an illegible scrawl competed for space with three by five cards, photos and a stale, gnawed bagel. "I've got seven weeks to finish—hell!—to write eleven chapters."

Sutherland's eyes widened. "Out of that rubble?"

"Yup."

He shook his head. "Always good at getting yourself in a bind, John." He smiled. "What's it about?"

Extracting a grainy eight by ten black-and-white glossy from the mess, he handed it to Sutherland. "It's about that debacle." Taken from a distance, the photo showed a charred, helmeted body amid the scattered ruins of shattered aircraft. All about, the stark Turanian Desert stood mute witness to chaos: weapons, radios, medical kits, intact choppers and code books littered the abandoned staging area.

"It has a title?" Sutherland asked with forced casualness, flipping the photo onto the desk.

"*Thy Banners Make Tyranny Tremble*. We're using that photo for the jacket."

"That's pretty damn cruel," snapped the CIA officer. "You know what happened. They cut and they cut and they cut until there was no redundancy—" He broke off, smiling ruefully. "Sorry, John. Old wounds. I'm sure it'll sell a million copies.

"As an alumnus you did clear this with us?"

"Harry Rosen in Liaison approved my sources and a brief outline."

Sutherland's eyes widened. "The Harry Rosen? 'No air cover' Rosen?" John nodded. "I'd heard he was running a catfish farm in Mississippi." He sipped his coffee.

"Okay, Bill," said John after a pause, "you didn't come here at the crack of dawn on a Sunday to shoot the breeze or drink day-old coffee. Level."

"I do have a small bit of nastiness that needs tending," he admitted. "As you knew when you saw my fine-chiseled face in your boob tube."

"I'd say 'blurring toward fat,' but go on."

"Any chance of Zahava's hearing this?"

John smiled. "No guarantee, but I'll try." Picking up the phone, he tapped a digit. A long moment later a mumble could be heard.

"Sorry to wake you, but Bill Sutherland's here and he wants to talk shop. Fine. Yeah, I'll tell him." He hung up.

"She'll be done in a few minutes. She says you're *meshuga*."

"Is that like crazy?" asked Sutherland, trying to kill the coffee's acridness with a dollop of cream. Even older than the coffee, it floated to the surface, small clusters of decay.

"That's like crazy."

Bill set the mug aside. "The cafeteria coffee's as lousy as when you left."

"Meaning?"

"Meaning, you can always have your old cubicle back. Same old gray metal desk with the 1942 coffee rings. Squeaky, green, vinyl-backed chair and basic black phone. And our current secretary's into primal scream."

"You make it sound so attractive."

Sutherland leaned forward, easing into his pitch. "It pains me to say it, but you're the best case officer I've had since . . . well, since I was a case officer."

It was, John realized as Bill continued, the classic Outfit pitch. The Russians are coming—to the wall, brothers! He interrupted with a laugh.

"I say something funny?" Sutherland glared.

"Bill, do you know how many times I've delivered that line? No, let me finish." He held up a hand. "I saved Uncle's ass a lot of times over the years. First with CIC in Asia, then with the outfit in Africa, and finally running your Eastern networks."

"Like I said, you were the best."

"Am the best. Good enough for the Outfit to pay me very well to bail it out, now and then. And when you're not in trouble, DIA or NSA is. It's a good living. I don't have to do it all the time, and I don't have to put up with bureaucratic b.s. So, William, save your pitch for the next candidate. I'm out.

"Whose ass needs saving today?"

Before Sutherland could reply, the door slammed back and a great white-haired bear of a man stormed in, wearing denim shirt and pants with red suspenders. Under his left arm was a star-spangled red, white, and blue motorcycle helmet.

"Can't ride a bike in this town without getting killed," he fumed. "Some turtlebrain's limo ran the light at Seventeenth and L. Another inch I'd have greased the road with my—" He spotted Sutherland.

"Bill! How's our merry master of mendacity?" He grinned.

"Bob—you unrepentant pinko." Sutherland shook the big hand. "Still riding that kraut suicide rack?"

"My daughter disapproves," the older man said with a smile. Sinking into an armchair, he plopped his helmet down on the blue-and-white Oriental. "But Jason and Melaine adore having the only grandpa in town with a two-wheeled BMW.

"What brings you over the bridge, Bill? Some lucrative chore we can perform?"

A lithe, olive-skinned woman in her late twenties came in, wet jet-black hair wrapped in a mauve towel, a man's red terry-cloth robe falling to her feet. Rather large feet, the CIA officer noted covertly.

"Good morning, Zahava," said Sutherland from the safety of his chair. He knew better than to rise for a sabra in the era of women's lib.

"Good morning," echoed John and McShane, also keeping their seats.

"Good morning," she said, pulling up a chair and lighting an unfiltered Camel. "This had better be worth my crawling out of bed, Bill."

"It's worth a listen, Zahava, believe me." He settled back in his chair, the center of attention. "First, though, the usual tired protocols." Taking a small voice-activated tape recorder from his pocket, he put it on the coffee table. "This briefing is classified Top Secret/Janissary. No one may reveal any portion of it without the prior written permission of the Central Intelligence Agency."

Stifling a yawn, Zahava poured herself a cup of coffee. They'd all heard this at least a dozen times in the past three years. She glanced at John, toying with his letter opener. Catching her eye, he gave her a lascivious wink.

"So much for that," said Sutherland. "Okay, here's the situation. Royal Petroleum's been trying to sink some test wells off the Massachusetts coast. The project is now a year behind. Supports for the first platforms haven't even been sunk. There may be as many as forty-eight billion barrels of oil out there, maybe five times that much in trillion cubic feet of natural gas."

"That would cut down on the filling station brawls, comes the next crunch," McShane said.

"And it would help hold the line till we diversify energy sources," said Sutherland.

"The delays, before last week, appeared to be coincidental: small accidents, bad hiring decisions, organizational snafus."

"Such as?" John asked.

"Oh, not ordering special equipment, damage to mapping gear, endless negotiations over the clearing and dredging of a modest port facility on Cape Cod.

"Royal's project crew is based at the Leurre Oceanographic Institute on Cape Cod. Last week they were finally set to begin seismic mapping and core sampling when the submersible *Argonaut* was lost with both divers. One of them was our man."

"This is domestic security," said John. "How did your people get into it?"

"*Argonaut* belonged to us. She was on loan to Leurre—

Leurre's under contract to Royal. We used her last year when we raised the *Ulianov*.'' It had been a brilliant CIA coup, that, raising a deep-sunken Soviet nuclear sub, her weapons, navigation and communications systems intact.

"What happened to the sub?" asked Zahava, tucking her feet beneath her on the chair.

"Lost. And our man murdered." Sutherland quietly put his coffee mug on the ceramic tabletop. "The body came drifting ashore at Yarmouthport. A poor attempt had been made to sink it. There was a speargun shaft through the heart."

"Anyone I knew?" asked John.

Sutherland shook his head. "No. Joe Antonucchi. Used to be in Reports, mostly West Africa. Just transferred in.

"He'd been investigating the delays for the past month. The night before he was killed, he met with an informant on the Institute staff. But we don't know who the informant was— Antonucchi never got to file a report."

"Any idea who's behind it?" asked Bob.

"We first assumed an unfriendly power, trying to restrict our energy resources. But that's changed. Take a look at this."

Sutherland opened his attaché case. Taking out a small flat package, wrapped in ordinary brown paper, he removed a triangular-shaped piece of rock, its edges fused. "This came, addressed to me, two days after we found Antonucchi's body," he said, passing the object to Bob. "The package had the right internal mail code. Joe's fingerprints were all over it."

McShane turned the fragment over in his large hands.

"What do you make of it, Bob?" asked Sutherland.

"I'm a political philosopher and historian, Bill," he replied, examining the marks chiseled into the front.

"But your hobby's Bronze Age languages, isn't it?"

"How much are you paying my grandchildren?" grumbled McShane, not looking up.

"You're a distinguished scholar, sir, your career one of public record," said Sutherland, velvet-voiced.

"Someday, someone is going to poison you, Bill, slowly," John said dryly.

Zahava peered over Bob's shoulder. "It looks like . . ."

"It is." The professor nodded. "The language Moses learned at the feet of the Great Ramses—Egyptian. Court Egyptian. It reads, 'The Exalted One: His Dwelling.'"

"Fascinating." He handed it to John, who glanced at it, then gave it back to Sutherland. The officer carefully re-wrapped it and locked it back in his attaché case.

"Good old igneous granite," Sutherland continued. "Found all over New England. Very rare on the Cape, though, but present."

"Why do you think it's from Cape Cod?" asked Zahava.

"Our resident geologists say it's from the northeastern United States. I believe Antonucchi sent it to me. He was on the Cape. I assume, therefore, that this three-thousand-year-old lettering is from Cape Cod."

"Are you sure it's not a forgery?" John asked, disbelieving.

"The stone and inscription are equally weathered."

"What is something from my part of the world doing in yours?" asked the Israeli.

"I'd have to brush up," Bob said, "but there's some evidence of pre-Columbian colonization of the Americas. Nothing as far back as this, though." He pointed to the attaché case. "But then, who knows?"

"Again, why us, Bill?" asked John. "I'm not trying to drive business away, but why not the FBI? A federal officer's dead."

"We're in a double bind, John. I shouldn't have sent Antonucchi in. And sure, legally it's a case for the FBI. The Bureau, though, tried to penetrate whatever's happening at the Institute for eight months. Nothing." He paused.

"The Bureau's come a million light-years since the overdue demise of the late Director. They're good people. I know—I work with them every day. And if I thought this a case requiring the wherewithal to walk unblinking into a firefight, I'd pick the Bureau over the Outfit any day. But this one's weird and political dynamite. If the Hill gets wind of our involvement in a domestic matter, it's good-bye Bill.

"So, I need you, the Outfit needs you, and, at the risk of being thought a jingoist, your country needs you. Or at least two of you. Zahava, think of it as indirectly helping Israel.

"Well?"

Bob raised his hand. "Aye."

"Why not," said Zahava, her hand joining McShane's in the air.

Shaking his head, John looked at the cluttered desk top. "Aye," he said with a sigh.

"Ah, I knew you couldn't let the Gipper down." Sutherland beamed. Rising, he switched off the tape recorder and pocketed it. "With your help, we'll get that port facility built and some producing wells dug. Can't run an armored division on cordwood."

He turned at the door. "I'll send a courier around with a full briefing packet.

"Oh, and John. Throw that coffee out. You'll live longer."

"Don't you feel Bill's just using us to get himself out of trouble?" asked Zahava over brunch the next morning.

John shrugged, looking up from the patio to the trees surrounding the townhouse's bricked-in yard. A pair of cardinals contended noisily with a blue jay for the last piece of winter suet hanging from the budding cherry tree.

"Yeah, probably. Don't complain, though. The last two assignments were easy money. Besides, it's often complex, sometimes intriguing work—even dangerous. Those are hard qualities to come by in a job these days. Especially one that pays as well as this."

"Israel doesn't lack for danger," she said pointedly.

"There you go, recruiting for the Mossad again." He smiled easily. Her glare vanished. "Look, again I promise—we'll live in Israel once we've enough money to be free of that horrible inflation rate."

It was a widening gap between them. Zahava had come to the States for the summer—several summers ago. John had met her in a grad seminar, learned of her Intelligence background and hired her to help out on a case. Despite their dissimilarities, they'd worked well together, become friends—close, intimate friends, much to the ill-concealed amusement of John's occasional helper, Bob McShane. After a year of living together, Zahava had extracted a reluctant promise from

John to return home with her when he graduated and if they had enough money. Well, he was graduating next month and they had enough money, but he didn't want to go.

He'd confessed to McShane—the Mideast with its insoluble carnage wasn't where he wanted to raise a family. But it was the only place Zahava would. Next month there'd be one very ugly confrontation.

"It's all arranged," called Bob, stepping onto the patio.

"What is?" John asked.

"Miss Tal's new career. Special Assistant to my old friend, Dr. Lawrence Levine. Larry's currently Director of Plankton Research at Leurre Oceanographic."

"I don't know anything about microorganisms, Bob!"

"Ah, but can you type?"

Agilely ducking the napkin ring, the professor sank into one of the white iron lawn chairs. Zahava menacingly hefted a grapefruit half.

"Peace, quarter!" McShane laughed, crossing his arms over his face. The grapefruit slowly returned to its bowl.

"Now listen, you two," he continued. "Zahava will have to type, marginally, but it's superb cover. Someone on the staff knows about that Egyptian stele and its origins. There are only about two hundred people at the Institute, and Oystertown's a small place."

"All right," conceded the Israeli.

"We're agreed, then? Zahava goes tonight? Larry will meet her at Hyannis Airport and see her to her motel." The two nodded.

"And tomorrow," John said, "I'll drop in on Fred Langston, the Institute's Director. I'm an investigator from Royal, checking into the project delays.

"And you're going to Boston?" he asked Bob.

"Yes. I've some related research to do, mostly at Harvard. I'll meet you two at your motel Wednesday."

"Sounds good."

"Typing—yeech." Zahava made a face, then raised her coffee cup. "Well, to a quick and successful investigation."

As the men lifted their cups, a lone mockingbird sang from the suet-hung tree.

*   *   *

John flicked on the Buick's headlights. The gray Cape Cod twilight found him alone on the two-lane road, flanked by scrub pine. The flight from National to Logan had been uneventful, only the cold driving rain marring his arrival.

Not chancing the box kite of a commuter plane that shuttled between Boston and Hyannis, he'd rented a car and was now nearing the end of a lonely drive down a nearly deserted Route 6, the only other traffic an occasional truck.

Wondering how Zahava had fared her first day at the Institute, his thoughts turned to dark, slender legs, supple thighs and sleepless, steamy nights in the big king-sized bed.

The tractor-trailer rig jackknifed across the road snapped him back to the present. Slowing to a stop, he saw no sign of a driver. Raincoat turned against the cold Atlantic drizzle, he got out and started toward the overturned cab, silently cursing the moron who'd evidently gone for help without setting flares.

Senses honed on a hundred night patrols saved him, sending him flying back behind the car as the bullets came, shattering the windows. Wrestling the big 9mm automatic from under his trench coat, John crawled toward the back of the car as the concealed gunman continued spraying the Buick.

Risking a quick look, he spotted the muzzle flash just as the rifle bolt snapped at the end of a magazine. Leaping up, he braced the pistol with both hands against the wet vinyl roof and emptied the weapon into the brush. Changing magazines, he charged across the slick road and into the bushes.

There was no one there, only spent shells and a small pool of viscous green liquid, melting away in the rain.

Shaken and angry, John returned to the car, checking tires and engine. They were okay, but the windows were mostly gone.

Breaking away the remaining fragments of windshield with the tire iron, he got in and drove slowly into the gathering dark, ignoring the rain that swept in, soaking him.

CHAPTER 3

JOHN GOT TO Oystertown just before five. Once a sleepy
Nantucket Sound fishing village, it had been transformed by
Leurre's endowers into a gentrified summer colony, a cob-
blestoned, yacht-slipped enclave for anyone with the money
and a taste for what the *Boston Globe* had dubbed Louisburg
Square-by-the-Sea.

Doric-columned brick townhouses lay astride pristine lanes
that ran like wheel spokes to Oystertown's centerpiece, a tidy
gaslit square and its tastefully tarnished bronze fountain, cast
as a vaulting dolphin.

The Institute fronted on the marina at the end of the square.
A rambling old brick-and-stone warehouse that had once stunk
of tar and salted fish, it had been gutted and rebuilt by the
Leurre Founder's Committee, a consortium of energy corpora-
tions. At one end was a small pub, at the other a cozy bistro,
Chez Nichée.

Dedicated to "Aid in the Exploration and Utilization of the
Oceans for the Betterment of Mankind," according to the brass
plaque set in the entrance way, the Institute served as a major
research facility for much of the nation's undersea energy and
mineral extraction.

Parking the shattered Buick under the "Visitors" sign, John
repaired himself as best he could, combing his hair, drying his
face and shucking his sodden raincoat.

Once in the foyer, the Institute's nineteenth-century mercan-
tile facade vanished, replaced by the gleaming modernity of
chrome and glass.

"Hello," he said to the lean, poker-faced guard behind the teak expanse of the security console. "I'm here to see Dr. Langston."

"Your name, sir." Black-uniformed, he expressionlessly took in John's dishevelment.

"Harrison. John Harrison."

"Just a minute, Mr. Harrison." He murmured softly into a small microphone, nodding to the voice that responded in his earpiece. "Please have a seat, sir. Dr. Langston will be right down."

Fred Langston was an affable, suave scientist-administrator. Fortyish, black, nattily attired, he quickly got John a fresh change of clothes, not questioning his story of a flat in the rain.

Seated in Langston's elegant office, John sipped a Scotch and water, admiring the small Klee above the fireplace.

The Director leaned back in his leather Scandinavian desk chair, quietly appraising Harrison. Behind him a big bay window overlooked the wharf, lit by antiqued gas lamps, and the dark sea beyond.

"Sutherland called me this morning," said Langston. "Warned me you'd be coming up today. He said you were an old friend who'd been retained by Royal. I wish I could be of more help, but"—he spread his hands helplessly—"you know as much about that man's murder as I do."

"Frankly, I'm only concerned with the murder because it may have some connection with the delays in the Royal project. Antonucchi's death makes the whole thing look like sabotage."

Langston nodded, toying with the dolphin-capped stirrer resting in his gin and tonic. "I know it does. At first we thought it was staff incompetence. No one's immune from personnel problems. So I had several people borrowed from Royal transferred back to Louisiana. Yet the problems continued. Then we lost *Argonaut*. Until we can get another submersible with her capabilities, we're stymied.

"If this is sabotage, Harrison, believe me, it's working. You can imagine how Royal is taking all this."

"Poorly, I'm told."

"Yes." He lightly drummed the stirrer on the rosewood

desk. "They're now seriously considering moving the entire operation to New Bedford, building the docking and refinery facilities there, rather than up the coast from here at Goose Cove.

"We could survive without Royal's contract and annual grant, but once one major corporation loses faith in you, it becomes pandemic. Old school tie, you know."

"May I look around, talk with your people?"

"Sure. But the state police and Sutherland's crew have gone all through that." He rose. "If I can be of any help, don't hesitate."

The rain had stopped. It made the short drive to the Beach-comber Motel cool but dry. A note in Zahava's hand awaited him at the desk.

John,

Registered here this A.M., but at lunch one of the staff invited me to stay with her. (Her boyfriend's been deported.)

Directions to an address in nearby Goose Cove Village followed.

Twenty minutes later he was knocking on the door of a cedar-shingled cottage on a quiet, pine-treed lot. A cute, bare-foot blonde in her midtwenties opened the door, wearing only shorts and a halter top despite the cold.

"Hi. You're John, aren't you. I'm Cindy.

"Zahava!" she called over her shoulder.

The Israeli, more practically outfitted in denim blouse and trousers, came in from the back screen porch. Planting a wet kiss on John's lips, she led him into the small living room. The decor was pure Sears, he noted with relief, still discomforted from Leurre's overpowering modernity. He sank into a battered armchair, the day finally catching up with him.

Cindy—Larry Levine's secretary—had met Zahava that morning and offered to share her rented house. She was still smarting from the loss of her previous roommate, Greg Farnesworth. Greg, the story came out over macaroni and cheese, was a geologist with Royal. He'd been on loan to the Institute for two months, till Fred Langston had cleaned house two weeks before. Greg had been abruptly returned to his home base in Shreveport.

After dinner, John walked Zahava out to the shattered rental car, parked beneath the pines. He quickly briefed her, adding, "I'm going over to the rental agency in Hyannis now to complain about vandals. I'd invite you along, but there's so much glass on the seats . . ."

"What about the man who tried to kill you?" she asked as he eased himself into the car.

"What man?" John said, shutting the door with a faint tinkle. "For all I know, it could've been the phantom of the opera. When I got there—ten seconds, maybe—he was gone. God only knows where. I should have bumped noses with him or at least seen him. All I saw was some M-sixteen brass and a sort of green ooze.

"I'd swear I hit the bastard, though." He started the engine. "And if blood were green, I'd know I did."

"Be back soon," she called as he drove off into the foggy night. He answered with a wave.

The rental manager didn't buy it. Belligerent, he was dialing the police when the account number on the contract caught his eye. Hanging up the phone, he shook his head. "You guys." He sighed.

Five minutes later, John pulled out in a new red Jeep. The manager inspecting the Buick looked up from his clipboard. "Let's see this one back in better shape, okay?" he called.

It took twice as long to get back to Goose Cove Village. The fog had closed in, making it hard to see beyond the headlights.

A new car was parked in front of the cottage; also a rental, John saw from the sticker.

Gathered on the comfortable old braided rug before a crackling fire was Zahava, Cindy and a sandy-haired man in his early thirties. The stranger drew his lanky frame up to greet John with a crisp, dry handshake.

"You must be John. I'm Greg Farnesworth."

"Up for the weekend?" John asked, joining them on the rug.

"For the week. Corporate largess," said the geologist

wryly, sipping his beer. "I took some vacation time to plead my case." He squeezed Cindy's knee.

She pouted, crinkling her freckles. "No Mom, no come." Her mother, she explained, lived alone in Boston, Cindy her only child.

"Okay," Greg said. "I'm buying a house, down on the bayou, complete with swamp and 'gators. There'll be a separate apartment for your mother, provided she comes to the wedding."

Cindy accepted with a hug and a kiss.

After hearty congratulations, toasted with brandy hoisted high in little paper cups, the topic turned to the Institute and Greg's job. He'd been in charge of surveying the Goose Cove site. The cove proper, as distinct from the village, was scheduled to be enlarged and dredged, serving as a port facility once the Georges Banks began producing.

"I'd gotten as far as sampling strata along Goose Hill—it overlooks the cove and was going to be blown up and carted away—when Langston suddenly declared me and my team bumblers and shipped us back to Shreveport inside of four hours." He sipped his brandy, staring pensively into the waning fire. Cindy put a comforting hand on his shoulder.

"Happily, there's a shortage of qualified petroleum geologists."

"You're still with Royal?" John asked.

"Yup. I leave on my schedule, not theirs."

"Why do you think Langston got rid of you?" asked Zahava.

"I think he was afraid of what I'd find up on that hill. Something that could end the entire operation, cause him to lose his grants, his imposing home, his nice office."

"And did you?" asked John.

The geologist gave him a hard look. "You're not working for Royal," he said flatly. "Not their type. Government?"

"Sort of."

Farnesworth nodded. "Yeah, I found it."

Before going to bed, John made two calls, one to Sutherland, the other to McShane in Boston.

CHAPTER 4

FOLLOWING JOHN'S DIRECTIONS, McShane had no trouble locating the dirt road leading from the paved, two-lane state highway to Goose Hill and the cove. He pulled into a small clearing among the bayberry and scrub pine at the foot of the hill. Parking next to a red Jeep, he made his way along the densely overgrown trail to the foot of the hill, brushing aside the morning's dew-covered cobwebs with his gnarled blackthorn Irish walker.

As he ascended, the trail quickly turned into a rocky defile, the undergrowth becoming sparser with each step. Passing between two boulders, he heard the soft snick of a well-oiled gun bolt sliding home. Taking a chance, he called, "Zahava! Don't shoot. It's kindly old Professor McShane."

Lowering her Uzi, she stepped from behind the right-hand boulder, all contriteness. "Bob! Are you okay? I hope I didn't frighten you."

"I am. You did not. When I was about your age, I was on a bloody isle called Tarawa. Nothing's frightened me much since then.

"Where is everybody?"

"Up ahead, in a maze of boulders. Greg . . ."

"The geologist John mentioned?"

"Yes. Greg's trying to find a particular rock."

"Appropriate for a geologist. Lead on."

They found the trio (Cindy having been ordered off to work, lest her absence arouse suspicion) on a shoulder of the hill, walking behind Greg as he slowly followed a map through a great tumbled-down pile of boulders. After quick introductions, he returned to his task as Bob quizzed John.

"Why in God's name did you drag me up here? I barely had time to finish at Harvard."

A triumphant "Eureka!" made them turn toward Greg, who was dancing an impromptu jig before a large, oblong outcropping that fell from the hill's brow to their feet.

"What's so unusual about that piece of granite?" demanded the professor, walking over to tap the rock with his stick.

"Several things," the geologist said with a smile, fondly stroking the outcropping. "One, it shouldn't be here. Granite in this quantity shouldn't occur on transient geological structures like this sandy peninsula. But we could probably explain it away, except that it isn't granite. Actually, it's not even rock. And I don't believe any of the hill is."

"Feels like rock," observed Bob, touching the surface.

Bowing, Greg extended his pickax. "Then perhaps you'd care to chip off a sample for analysis?"

Rising to the bait, Bob took the tool and swung hard at a rounded edge. There was no visible effect. Mumbling, "Obdurate matter," he handed his stick to John. Seizing the pick with both hands, he braced his legs, aimed carefully, and swung at the offending rock with all of his not inconsiderable bulk. The pick rebounded, resonating. Yelping, Bob dropped the tool, hands still stinging from the shock. His target shone unblemished in the morning light.

"I yield," he said with more humility than either John or Zahava had ever heard. "What is it?"

"Well," said Greg, recovering the pick, "according to spectrum analysis of a small portion—which I got after three hours' work with a laser torch—it's an alloy with the density of titanium, but ten to the fourth times titanium's tensile strength.

"I have no idea what it *is*, though. Nor does the lab that ran the tests.

"But now for the pièce de résistance." He took a flashlight from his small day pack. "I stumbled onto this while playing the laser over the surface." Flicking on the beam, he flashed it onto a dark upper corner of the outcropping, a spot the sun never touched. A tiny green flash responded.

The lower quarter of the outcropping noiselessly detached itself from the rest of the great slab, swinging aside. A neatly finished opening, the width of two men, lay before them. Dust-laden stairs dropped into the hill's stygian interior. Two sets of bootprints, one up and one down, spoke of recent entry.

For a long moment only the sound of wind and surf playing against the weather side of the hill was heard.

"The implications of this find, if it's what I believe, are so vast, so sweeping . . ." Bob said, a quiver in his voice.

"You ain't seen nothing yet," drawled Greg.

"Yours?" John asked, pointing to the bootprints.

"From the day before my banishment. Care for a tour?"

"Someone should stand guard." John carefully avoided Zahava's glare. "Hate to get trapped down there."

Relenting only after heavy pleading, she went—pouting—to a point commanding the trail.

Greg led the way with his flashlight, followed by McShane. John brought up the rear.

Harrison counted 150 steps down. Then the rock-hewn passage turned sharply right, widening into a vaulted chamber, its center dominated by a rough stone altar. The walls tiered upward into equally rude stone benches. In all, John guessed, the small chamber might have held fifty people.

"Do you know what this is?" asked Greg, his tone implying they didn't.

"It would appear to be an altar chamber sacred to Bel of the Celtiberians—the Celtic peoples," Bob said evenly. He played his own light, suddenly materialized from a baggy tweed pocket, over the oval altar stone.

"I expected something like this, Greg—I've been doing some reading. This chamber could probably be dated around 100 A.C.E., if certain conflicts didn't exist."

"Such as?" asked John, knowing of at least one: sophisticated technology guarding the entrance to a rude temple contemporary with Christ.

"Principally this," said Bob, holding up the stone fragment John had last seen disappearing into Sutherland's briefcase. "I had to sign my life away to get this from Bill. As we know, it's Egyptian of the Middle Kingdom. It fits perfectly, I'll bet, into that freshly carved niche over the outside entrance way. Your work?'' he asked Greg.

"Yes." The geologist nodded. "I gave it to Joe Antonucchi the night before I was shipped out. I see he managed to get it off before he was killed.

"A killing, by the way, I only heard about from Cindy a week after it happened."

"You're clean," said John. "The FBI placed you in Shreveport that day.

"So, you think this is what got Antonucchi killed?"

"Sure do," Greg said. "Once this find was announced, no port facility, no more Royal contract. Would've put a crimp in Freddy's life-style."

"Wrong," said Bob. "If I were Langston, I'd give my right hand to have found this. I'd be honored by my colleagues—once they got over the shock. Any university in the world would have had me, on my own terms." Silhouetted by Greg's powerful light, he leaned against the altar.

"Besides," John added. "Royal wouldn't cancel Leurre's contract. They'd just move the docking facility to New Bedford and bask in the sheen of Langston's reflected glory. Think of the PR."

Greg nodded. "I see your point."

"Any thoughts on the doorway?" asked McShane.

"A million." Farnesworth grinned. "All culled from Saturday sci-fi reruns. I do have an observation, though. Even under a magnifying glass, there's no visible separation between rock and door. They seem melded together—maybe on a sub-molecular level."

Bob cleared his throat. "I see. Well, that does steal some of my thunder."

"We interrupted you," said John. "I'm sorry. You were saying about the fragment?"

"I was saying that the fragment is in a language whose peoples were dust five thousand years before the Celts of Europe. There are lucid arguments for the existence of ancient trading routes to the New World from the classical—Egypt,

Tarshish, Carthage. Dead Mediterranean languages have been found carved into rocks throughout North America, especially New England. But this is the first evidence that allegedly unrelated, loose trading confederations not only were established on these shores, but overlapped, interacting with each other down through time. To believe that two people so far separated in time and origin as the Celts and the Egyptians occupied the same concealed site—concealed, mind you!—fifty centuries apart through coincidence . . . well, I can't accept it. The little green light and its wondrous door only fuel my skepticism."

Machine-gun fire echoed thinly through the temple.

"Zahava!" cried John, leading the rush for the stairs.

CHAPTER 5

THE ISRAELI HAD been settled behind some boulders no more than ten minutes when movement in the undergrowth below snapped her to the alert.

A score of Institute security guards, carrying M-16s, were winding their way up the trail toward her, led by Fred Langston. When they were out of the brush, about forty yards away, she shouted, "Halt!" and fired a warning burst.

All but Langston dived for cover. "Hold your fire!" he shouted. "Harrison, is that you?"

"His associate," Zahava called back.

"I'm unarmed and coming up alone." Which he did, topping the rough trail quickly, without visible exertion.

"Where's Harrison," he demanded, ignoring the Uzi's muzzle leveled at his belly.

"Here." John appeared from behind the boulders.

"How ya doin', Freddy?"

"Farnesworth!"

Langston turned angrily to John. "Harrison, this area's strictly off limits. We're doing some very delicate work up here. No trespassers."

"I thought I had carte blanche, Langston."

"Certainly, as relates to *Argonaut* and the murder. But this is totally unrelated. I insist you leave now."

"And if we don't?"

"I'll be forced to expel you." He emphasized "expel."

"How did you find us, Dr. Langston?" Bob asked, surveying the guards deploying along the hillside. "Just happen to be out grouse hunting with this little task force and stumble over us?''

"We have an excellent security system.''

"One more appropriate to the Manhattan Project," said John. "Once I make a few phone calls, Langston, expect a visit in force from the FBI. I'd like to hear you explaining your need for automatic weapons.''

"You have three minutes to be on your way." Turning, he started back down the trail.

"Hey, Freddy, I found it," Greg said, leaning insouciantly against a boulder. Langston froze for an instant, then resumed walking, seeming not to have heard.

"Take cover," John said. "It's their move." He joined Zahava behind the rocks, pistol drawn.

The guards had used the time to find better positions. Reaching them, the Director barked an order, diving for cover.

A hail of M-16 slugs ricocheted off the rocks. The barrage was so intense that John and Zahava couldn't return the fire. It was only a matter of moments until a bullet would find one of the four.

Turning to gauge a possible retreat over the hilltop, John saw two black-uniformed figures low-crawling along the crest. Sighting carefully, he snapped off five quick shots.

One man rolled backward, out of sight, his short, blunt weapon clattering down the hill. The other beat a hasty retreat.

"Cover me!" Greg shouted above the din. As John and Zahava drew the guards' fire, the geologist scampered out onto the trail and back again, clutching his prize: the fallen man's weapon.

"M-Seventy-Nine grenade launcher," he panted, breaking open the breach. "Haven't seen one of these since 'Nam." He snapped the weapon shut.

"We can't stay here and we can't retreat," said John, reloading his pistol. "Can you use that?"

"I can put one right in their laps.''

"Bob, when you hear the detonation, you and Greg run for the passageway. Zahava and I'll cover.''

McShane nodded curtly.

"Now!''

Sighting carefully, Greg fired. The grenade exploded between two of Langston's men, hurling them into the scrub. John and Zahava emptied their magazines into the guard force. Weak, ineffectual fire responded.

"Let's get out of here!" They ran after the others.

"Where's Bob?" John asked Greg, waiting for them inside the open entrance.

"In the altar chamber. Wait a sec, I'll close this." He shined his light at a point inside the doorway parallel to the sensing device on the outside. The rock swung silently shut. Descending to the altar chamber, they found Bob busily examining the altar.

"Think they'll follow?" asked Zahava.

"No. Langston obviously knows what's here and how to get in. And he knows we'd slaughter his men in that narrow passageway."

"Now what?" Greg asked as he and John sat on a bench, sharing a canteen. "You're the specialist."

John shrugged. "If we wait, maybe they'll go away. Unless you've a better suggestion."

"Inspiring."

"Come, come, Greg," said Bob, looking up from the pedestal. "We're doing very well. In one day we've uncovered the villain, made archaeological history and stood off a band of desperados. Now all we have to do is get out alive."

"You can continue your briefing now, Bob," John said. "We're not pressed for time."

"My pleasure." He sat atop the altar, legs crossed, stick by his side. "Let me recap for Zahava what happened while she was topside." Which he did, continuing in his best seminar manner, "So finding this site creates more mysteries than it solves. We can credit, given the mass of conventionally ignored evidence lying about the New World, that there was a great deal of pre-Columbian exploration of the Americas, stretching from the ancient Mediterraneans forward to the Celts at about the time of Caesar.

"The Celts, by the way, were superb mariners. Caesar himself says so in the third book of his *De Bello Gallico*, the *Gallic Commentaries*.

"Trade between this continent and Europe, we may speculate, effectively ended with the rise of Roman might. The colonists were then absorbed by the 'natives,' themselves the children of previous colonies, their heritage long forgotten. From these peoples came the various Amerindian tribes.

"That, at least, is how archaeology, once it confronts this find, will explain it. What it will not, cannot, explain is the concealment of this site by a sophisticated technology—one possibly in advance of our own and evidently dating from the site's construction.

"Equally bizarre is the seemingly successive sharing of this site by the diverse peoples who touched these shores. Such a technology, such an artful melding of different cultures, bespeaks a sophisticated guiding force, a mentor, stretching forth its hand through the centuries.

"Who built this place and why? How many different feet have trod here? And, more pressing, why is Langston so determined to keep this a secret? I'm sure it has nothing to do with his career goals."

"Aren't you leaping rather quickly to conclusions, Professor?" asked Greg.

"What's your alternative? Piltdown Man, the Hitler diaries, an elaborate hoax?"

Greg nodded.

Bob smiled, shaking his head. "By whom—to what end? Every effort's been made to conceal this place, not to foist it on the academic community. Also, and this is intangible, it *feels* old."

He was right. They all felt it, an aura of antiquity pervading the altar, the stone tiers, the tunnel and stairs worn smooth by feet eons dust.

"'The dark and backward abysm of time,'" John quoted softly.

The heavy thud of explosions rocked their sanctuary, sending them diving to the hard floor amidst a shower of falling rock.

"They're blowing their way in!" Greg shouted as the din continued.

"No." John picked himself up as quiet returned. "I think they've sealed us in."

A quick trip up to the entrance proved him right. There was no winking green light. The door would't budge under their combined efforts.

"Clever," said Zahava. "Letting our thirst kill us."

Somber, they rejoined Bob. Seemingly undeterred by the prospect of a lingering death, he was still exploring the altar by the fading beam of his light.

"There's got to be another way out," said John, shining his own light along the chamber walls.

"No, there doesn't," said Bob. "But in fact, there is. *Voilà!*" He rose from his knees before the altar as the massive capstone swung soundlessly aside. A ladder of gleaming alloy, fastened to the side of the altar well, plunged into the dark beyond the range of their lights.

"Curiouser and curiouser," Bob mumbled, lowering himself gingerly onto the top rung. "What are you waiting for?" he growled as they hesitated. "We'll be as dead as this place is if we don't find another exit."

One after another, they followed him down into the blackness.

CHAPTER 6

"AND SO?" demanded Sutherland, his voice tinny in the pay phone receiver.

"Down the ladder, into a tunnel like the first one," John said. Greg, Zahava and Bob sat behind him in the small diner, sipping coffee. "The tunnel was indirectly lit, power source unknown.

"Past a locked door—same alloy as the ladder—about a half mile farther. Another quarter mile and we came to a light-activated entrance like the one Langston's crew sealed. We found ourselves on the weather side of Goose Hill, just above the breakwater. Bob marked the spot with his walking stick.

"We followed the beach several miles to South Dunsmore—a delight on a cold night with the tide running high. We're now feasting on greaseburgers in the aptly named Clam Shack."

"Langston thinks you're still down there?"

"Evidently."

"Incredible." Sutherland paused, collecting his thoughts. "I'm coming down with a team tomorrow morning. I'll have FBI Liaison with me and a pocketful of John Doe warrants. Meet me at Otis Air Force Base at oh-six-hundred. Lay low till then."

John returned to the others and a now cold cheeseburger. "He's coming down first thing tomorrow," he said to the expectant faces. "We're to meet him at Otis."

"I'd like to get a good look at that site before then," Bob said between mouthfuls of blueberry pie. "Once the Outfit's

36

house staff gets in there, all data will be tucked away in secret archives for centuries."

"We could walk back down the beach," suggested Greg.

"I'd like to try to open that locked door," Zahava said.

"I second that." John rose, throwing a few bills on the table. "I don't relish facing the cold wind and spray, though," he admitted, sliding from the booth.

"Salubrious—builds character," said McShane, gulping down his coffee. With a pleasant "Thank you" to the waitress, he followed his friends into the chill night.

Taking a chance that Tuckman was still in, Sutherland dialed his office. Despite the hour, the Director was there, answering his own phone. Bill quickly sketched the day's events at Goose Hill, concluding, "I'd like to take a team down there tomorrow morning, sir. It would include FBI CIC Liaison, so we'd be on firm legal ground."

"Do that, Bill," said Tuckman. "But make sure that any arrests are made by the Bureau. I'm due before the Senate Select Committee on Intelligence next month." It was budget time. "If this excursion comes back to haunt us, we may both be counting yaks in the Himalayas as grade nothings. Clear?"

"Perfectly."

"Good luck. Call me from the Cape."

Ringing the duty watch, Sutherland had calls put out for his team with instructions to meet him at Andrews Air Force Base by midnight. He then called Emmy-chan, his Eurasian friend, if "friend" is the word for someone you've lived with for twelve years.

She took it with a stoicism born of necessity and sustained by love, telling him, as always, "Come back to me." As always, he said he would. Going out to his car, he headed for the Beltway and Andrews.

"The more I see of this tunnel, the more it puzzles me." Bob's voice echoed down the passageway. They were approaching the door they'd passed during their escape. A diffuse golden glow bathed the corridor.

"The lights seem to come on whenever anyone enters," said John.

"Then there's a functioning power source," Zahava said. "But how could any piece of equipment operate through all the centuries this place's been abandoned?"

"Note the walls," said McShane, running his hand along the surface. "Rock, but with the texture of glass. Not a chisel mark, no sign of power tools. Far better than anything our technology's capable of."

"Someday we'll replicate this, Bob." Greg spoke for the first time since they'd left the beach. "When we finally translate particle beam theory into hardware. This is star wars stuff—applied atomics." Gone was the laid-back, mint-julep-and-magnolia accent.

They stood before the door, an oval slab of metal flush with the wall. Greg flashed his light expectantly at the usual place. Nothing happened. "Any ideas?" he asked, flicking the torch off.

"There is something here, I think," said John. "May I?" Canting the beam, barely grazing the space just above the door, he brought out the hieroglyphics, invisible in the corridor light. "Can you read that, Bob?"

"Yes, but I don't see how it helps. It says, 'Tell who you are and why you come.'"

They stood mute for a moment, then John snapped his fingers. "Tolkien!"

Loudly, he said, "John Harrison and a party of three. We're exploring this installation, which we believe abandoned."

"'Speak "friend" and enter,'" Greg recalled softly as the door disappeared. A refined contralto voice filled the corridor. "Please come in."

Hesitantly, John leading, they stepped down into a high-ceilinged room no larger than the altar chamber. Silently, the door closed behind them.

Several compact consoles occupied the half of the room nearest the door. Their control panels flickered into life.

"Please proceed to the empty area fronting the equipment," directed the voice.

"Who are you?" Zahava demanded, unslinging the Uzi. She spat an Arabic curse as the gun vanished.

A high-pitched whine filled the room, rising quickly to

mind-searing intensity. Futilely clapping their hands over their ears, they dropped to the floor, writhing in agony, eyes bulging, screaming unheard into the merciless pitch.

Abruptly, the killing noise stopped.

"When you have recovered," the voice kept repeating, "please proceed to the area in front of the equipment." Helping each other, they stumbled forward, obeying.

"Thank you."

They were gone. The room was empty.

Soon all the lights dimmed out, and the centuries resumed their slow, silent passage.

Boarding the sleek little corporate jet, Sutherland exchanged nods with his three team members. Marsh and Johnson were CIA; Tim Flannigan, now buried in a sports magazine, was FBI Liaison, the only one with arrest authority.

Heading forward to brief the pilot, Sutherland spotted an unfamiliar man sitting away from the others. Something about the man tugged at his memory; thin, almost ascetic features, high forehead, thinning blond hair. Looks like a Jesuit, he thought.

As he approached, the stranger glanced up, recognition in his cool gray eyes. A hand fell on Bill's shoulder, and he turned away from those eyes.

"Tuckman!" No mistaking the elegant features and silver hair.

"None other," the Director said with a smile.

"What are you doing here, sir?" Sutherland asked, sensing deviousness on a large scale.

"All in good time, Bill. Let me introduce our guest."

The stranger rose, stepping into the aisle. "Deputy Director Bill Sutherland, may I present Colonel Andreyev Ivanovich Bakunin—André—of the Second Chief Directorate of the—"

"KGB," said Sutherland coldly. "The man responsible for the destruction of our network within Solidarity and the deaths of ten good—"

"Traitors," the Russian interrupted evenly. "Ten good traitors, Mr. Sutherland. They sold the revolution, the revolution repaid them. To each according to his worth." His accent was cosmopolitan.

"Sir," Sutherland said angrily, turning to Tuckman, "I protest the presence of a Soviet officer—"

"Enough, both of you." The Director reached past Bakunin, picking up a handset. "Jensen," he said to the pilot, "let's roll. Call me when we're ten minutes from Otis.

"Strap in, gentlemen," he ordered as the jets whined higher. "I'll hold mission briefing when we're airborne."

A few minutes later, when all were seated around the conference pit to the plane's rear, sipping coffee, Tuckman began, glancing occasionally at his notes. "In 1944, on the south coast of France, a German raiding party swept into a cave. They believed the cave to be a Resistance staging area. Too late, they discovered their mistake."

"Something unpleasant happen to them, sir?" asked Yazanaga, the team's technical specialist.

"Wiped out. By particle beam weapons." He said it casually, taking a croissant from the coffee table.

"Sir," said Marsh into the uneasy silence, "particle beams were science fiction back then—mostly still are." He glanced uneasily at the expressionless Russian. An analyst of Soviet military technology, Frank Marsh knew of the long-term Russian research in laser and particle beams.

"Colonel Bakunin," said Tuckman, deferring to the Russian.

The KGB officer cleared his throat. "I am authorized to tell you that the radiation traces still in that cave, and at the other sites, are very similar to the residue from our own particle beam testing."

My God! thought Bill. Whatever the hell's going on must have scared the Presidium down to its toenails for that to come out. Before he could ask what other sites, Tuckman continued.

"Some years after the war, an SS officer sold us a map, a very odd map captured by a mortally wounded Abwehr officer during that raid. It sketched the world as we knew it, except for the Antarctic, which was shown without its ice covering. The accuracy of that was only confirmed in the late 1950's by satellite photogammetry. The map's lettering was in a language or code NSA's been unable to crack. It was impregnated into a thin, pliable, highly durable polymer that continues to defy analysis.

"Also on the map, scattered over the globe, are two hundred and fifty-eight red Xs, usually along the coast or well inland. Although it's a very large scale map, one of the marks is plainly on the south coast of France. Proceeding logically, we began the task of finding the other sites. As the French site was underground, we assumed the others would be. We thought we'd gotten lucky after a few months—a cave in Oregon. But like the French site, whatever had been there was destroyed. Just fused lumps of metal congealed on the floor. A small place, really, just a few tunnels hollowed out of bedrock, a cleverly concealed entrance. Analysis of the metal showed the presence of alloys unknown to us—alloys not composed of any known elements."

"Excuse me, sir," said Flannigan. "Did you say no known elements?"

The Director nodded, pausing to sip coffee. "Operations were stepped up.

"The Soviets got their map the same time we did. It was a copy, sold them by the same ex-SS."

"There is no such thing as an ex-SS," said Bakunin.

"Anyway, the Soviets did not begin looking until shortly after we found another site in Montana and lost our team—also to particle beam fire. Shortly after that, the KGB very quickly found a site near Batumi, on the Black Sea. They lost their team, too.

"That was ten years ago. Since then there's been close cooperation on this between myself and General Branovsky, Head of the Second Chief Directorate. Characteristically, the Soviets consider this a problem of internal security, so Second Directorate's in charge. As it was first thought a foreign intelligence matter for the U.S., I was given the assignment, initially reporting to then-Director Mr. Dulles. Currently I report to the President's National Security Advisor, José Montanoya.

"Colonel Bakunin was in Washington to discuss progress with me when your call came, Bill. We drew certain conclusions and here we are.

"Floor's now open for discussion."

His men looked to him, waiting. Sutherland voiced it for all of them. "You're talking about an . . . outside force, sir, aren't you? Something with a technology way ahead of ours. Something keenly interested in finding those sites and preventing us from finding them?"

"Little green gremlins," said the Director. "That's what President MacDonald calls them. Lord knows, he may be right."

"If teams have been wiped out," Bill asked, "why aren't we going in with an armored division?"

"Armored divisions attract attention, Bill. And they're no protection against little green gremlins with, how to say, blasters?

"There was a movie some years ago, *The Andromeda Strain*. Everyone see it?" Sutherland was surprised when Bakunin nodded with the rest. "You'll recall, then, that when something lethal and alien falls from the skies, the team sent in after it was considered expendable. We're expendable, gentlemen. But then that's always gone with the territory, hasn't it?" He poured more coffee.

It was a long while before anything but the steady throbbing of the jets broke the silence.

CHAPTER 7

"THE SHIELD IS fully operational, Captain," said N'Trol. Wiry, middle-aged, with the deep-seamed tan that comes from a lot of years hullside, the Engineer had come to the bridge to make his report. He looked tired.

D'Trelna grinned a smug little grin. "Thank you, Mr. N'Trol. Care for a t'ata?" The Engineer nodded. "Sit, sit." The Captain waved to the empty flag-officer's station at his rear, swiveling about as N'Trol sat. D'Trelna handed him the steaming cup that appeared atop the chair arm, dialing up another for himself.

"You've done a great job, Engineer. My compliments to you and your staff." N'Trol nodded, acknowledging with an all but imperceptible smile as he sipped the t'ata. "We no longer have to worry about S'Cotar flitting aboard. I'm not aware of anything but massed fusion or missile fire having ever penetrated a Class One Imperial Shield."

"True, sir. A telekinetic beam scatters against a shield like sand against a wall." He finished the drink. "With your permission, sir, I'd like to get some sleep."

"With my blessing. Go."

As N'Trol left, D'Trelna turned back around. "Time to planet three, Mr. K'Raoda?"

"Shield penetrated!" L'Sura cried. Alarms hooted as he pointed midway between Navigation and Weapons. "Life forms materializing . . . there!"

"Shipwide," snapped the Captain. "Intruders on bridge. Controls to auxiliary. Reaction force to bridge. Battlestations! Battlestations!" The battle klaxon joined the security alarms.

43

D'Trelna moved fast. Even as a searing white light burst over the bridge, he was on his feet, squinting against the fierce glare, listening for one more alarm before he pulled the trigger.

When spots stopped dancing before their eyes, the K'Ronarins saw four very bewildered humans standing next to Navigation. The bridge S'Cotar detectors remained silent.

"Hold fire," ordered D'Trelna. "They're not transmutes. Identify yourselves!"

The oldest of the four, a big, white-haired man, fell to his knees, gasping. "Bob!" cried John. He and Zahava knelt beside the professor as K'Raoda called, "Medtech to the bridge." Stripping off his field jacket, Greg bundled it under Bob's head.

The reaction force burst in, D'Nir at their head. The sergeant looked disappointed at the absence of S'Cotar.

"Get them off the bridge, Sergeant," said D'Trelna as a medtech brushed past him to tend McShane.

"Let go of me," snapped Harrison as a commando grabbed his arm, trying to pull him away from Bob. Zahava rose, seeming to comply, then drop-kicked D'Nir, only to have her arms pinioned.

"This is absurd," D'Trelna said, stepping down from the command tier and past the doubled-over NCO. "Commandos, stand clear. D'Nir, you should be ashamed of yourself, sap-kicked like that.

"Well?" he asked Q'Nil, the medtech.

The man looked up, putting away the diagnoster. "Shock, minor stroke. Their heart and respiratory systems seem slightly different from ours. A while in sick bay and he should be fine." Filling a hypo, he pantomimed injecting Bob, looking questioningly at the three other Terrans. They nodded.

"We've got to communicate," said D'Trelna. "D'Nir, very calmly, without injuring yourself further, escort the two men and the woman to Briefing Room Three, Five Deck. K'Raoda, have Survey bring five cerebral translators there on the run." As he spoke, McShane's breathing eased and he slept.

Reassured by D'Trelna's crude sign language that Bob would be all right, the trio went reluctantly with the commandos. As they left, two crewmen arrived, wheeling a medcart.

"Where are we?" Zahava asked in a tiny voice as the lift angled down and across the ship.

"You're asking me?" said John nervously. "Wherever we are, though, how'd we get here? One instant we're under Cape Cod, the next—zap!—we're in this great gray metal womb."

"And who are these guys," asked Greg, "the lost space patrol?" He glanced at the four commandos. Stringently obeying D'Trelna's order, they stood to one side of the big lift. Young, in top shape, wearing brown lightweight tunics with matching trousers, short haircuts and big black belts on which were holstered the long, wide-bore pistols the Terrans had been staring into on the bridge, the troopers looked very much like a space patrol.

Exiting, the trio were hurried down a long gray corridor, arriving shortly at an austere room: black metal table with matching straight-backed chairs and four blank, gray walls.

D'Trelna and L'Wrona arrived a moment later. The latter took a double handful of small, black boxes from a crewman, placing them on the table.

Snapping one of them open, the K'Ronarin officer removed what looked like a tiny, one-piece hearing aid. Placing it in his right ear, he gestured for the Terrans to do the same. When they hesitated, D'Trelna selected a box at random and imitated L'Wrona's action.

After they'd all adjusted their translators, the Captain asked, "Can you understand me?"

"Yes."

"Do you know where you are?"

"No," said John tersely. "Who are you?"

"I am Captain J'Quel D'Trelna, commanding the K'Ronarin Confederation starcruiser *Implacable*. This is Commander H'Nar L'Wrona, my Executive Officer."

"Starcruiser?" John asked, a catch to his voice. "Can you prove it?"

L'Wrona pushed a button. A wall opaqued into transparency. They stared, gasping, as the light of a billion billion stars flooded the room.

"We're closing on what we believe to be your home world," said D'Trelna, staving off a barrage of questions.

L'Wrona pressed another button. Space vanished, replaced

by a close-up of an almost cloudless Western Hemisphere. "Is that your home planet?" asked the Captain.

"That's it," John said. "Where are we?"

"We're halfway between your home—what do you call it?"

"Terra."

"We're halfway between Terra and your system's fourth world," explained D'Trelna. "We're decelerating, so it'll be some hours before we're within range."

L'Wrona switched the wall back to space view.

"Range?" said Zahava with quiet alarm.

"I'm sorry," the Captain apologized. "A poorly chosen word. Landing range. We intend to land a scout craft and explore your specific point of origin, as traced by ship's computer."

"Just why did you bring us here, Captain, and how?" demanded John, his face pale and angry.

"We did not bring you, sir. You were thrust upon us—we suspect by matter transport, a technology lost to us. And one we need very badly.

"We're in your system to investigate a report of extant Imperial technology," continued D'Trelna, leaning back in his chair. Taking in their puzzled faces, he smiled.

"I see I'm going too fast. Let's begin with basics. You know our names. What are yours?"

John introduced his friends, adding, "We're tired, hungry and more than a little confused."

"I can take care of the first and second items," said L'Wrona, dialing up four steaming platters of food and equally hot cups of beverage from a wall unit. "And I hope we can resolve our mutual confusion," he said, placing the food before *Implacable*'s guests and resuming his seat.

"This is delicious," enthused Zahava, digging into meaty stew.

"As to 'mutual confusion,'" D'Trelna said. The wall now displayed a three-dimensional star map: several score points of white light, scattered among three roughly equal colored zones—blue, green and yellow.

"The Confederation of K'Ronarin Republics as it was a decade ago. Three semiautonomous states, descendants of the strongest of the old Imperial sectors, united for trading and mutual defense.

"The Confederation as it is today."

Half of the map now shone scarlet.

"Ten years ago we harbored the dangerous belief that we were alone in the galaxy," said L'Wrona, picking up the tale. "Our ancestors, whose Empire charted half our galaxy, found only fossils in their search for other sentient life.

"Then the S'Cotar swept in on us from the barren marches of space. The red is theirs by right of conquest." His tone was bitter.

"The S'Cotar," added D'Trelna, "are a voracious, telepathic insectoid. Origin—unknown. History—unknown. Ultimate purpose—unknown. Captives destroy themselves quickly and nastily—a bomb in the brain.

"We do know, however, that they consist of two castes."

The map vanished, replaced by a six-legged insectoid. It stood erect on four long legs, its upper two limbs each splayed into four tapered tentacles. The tentacles were firmly wrapped about a strange, long-barreled rifle. Bulbous red eyes and a pair of jutting, serrated mandibles lent the creature a hellish cast. John suppressed a shudder.

"Warrior," said the Captain. "You can't tell from the projection, but that little beauty stands six feet tall, can outrun a man, can live on nothing for weeks and will eat anything, including and especially humans."

What looked like a large praying mantis now stood before them. "Command caste," L'Wrona explained. "Unlike the warrior, it has telepathic abilities. It can transport itself and a number of warriors over vast distances. It can assume human guise and adapt to human conventions—well enough to infiltrate the hierarchy of an entire planet."

L'Wrona turned away from the projection. "An ability, by the way, initially and incorrectly defined as transmutation. The term stuck and has since become a noun. We first thought you were transmutes.

"When the S'Cotar attack, key people vanish, contradictory orders are given and planetary defenses quickly fall. The red bulge extends further into the Confederation. That's been the fate of twenty-three planets in the past ten years.''

"You say you're here searching for the remains of your Empire's technology," said Zahava. "What sort of technology? And why?''

"Excuse me," D'Trelna said, reaching in front of his XO. "Something more pleasant, I think." The S'Cotar disappeared, replaced by the original star view.

"We're looking for an intact Imperial transporter web—they had them on all their Colonial Service bases. With it, we could overcome the S'Cotar's telekinetic edge.''

"We look for anything, though," said L'Wrona. "The war's turned us into galactic scavengers. This ship, for example, dates from the Fall—the fall of the Empire—five thousand years ago. She was found in a stasis cache beneath a gutted Imperial fleetbase. Much of her equipment is Imperial.

"These warsuits," he continued, indicating the shiny, form-fitting jumpsuits he and the Captain wore, "are Imperial. They'll absorb all but the most concentrated blaster fire and double as hard vacuum suits. They were only recently found in an automated warehouse on K'Ronar, misrouted there centuries ago and forgotten. Today they took hostile fire for the first time in five thousand years.''

"If they hadn't, we would have," D'Trelna said. "You'd have arrived during my funeral." He smiled humorlessly.

"And these?" Greg tapped his earpiece.

"Imperial," said L'Wrona. "We're not sure, but we think they send, receive and correlate thought patterns. We *do* know that they firmly instill the alien language in the wearer's mind." He paused, taking in their unbelieving faces.

"Oh, it's true," D'Trelna affirmed. "In a few days you won't need the translators.''

"I gather you plan on our company for a while, then, Captain?" asked John.

D'Trelna smiled. "You listen well, Mr. Harrison. Yes, for a few days, no more. Then, I hope, we can all go our separate ways. Provided events don't overtake us.''

"What events, Captain?" asked Greg.

"There are S'Cotar in this solar system—we've already

been attacked. And why you're still alive, I don't know," he added, catching their exchange of alarmed glances. "Their usual pattern would have been to purge your planet of you, then expropriate your resources. Although, as Commander L'Wrona told you, sometimes the S'Cotar will infiltrate a planet, toppling it from within even as their fleet attacks. What happens then isn't known—not one of our scouts has ever made it back."

John spoke into the silence. "Why do you need us at all, Captain?"

"The only technology we know," replied the officer, "that could have punched a hole in our Class-One Imperial shield and reassembled your atoms on my deck is an Imperial transport system. One directed by a Colonial Service computer—at least a POCSYM Three. Therefore, I look to the origin of your trip here to find that badly needed transporter."

He paused as comprehension dawned on the Terrans' faces, then continued slowly, deliberately. "We could just blast in and find it, you know. We'll have your point of origin by now and *Implacable* is more than a match for your planet's combined defenses.

"But"—he held up a hand as John's face clouded angrily—"not only is it against our law, but human life is becoming a rarity in the universe. So I can't, won't, demand. I ask. Will you help us?" His voice held a certain tenseness.

John scanned his friends' faces, then turned back to D'Trelna. "We'll be happy to help in any way we can, Captain."

"Thank you," said D'Trelna, relaxing with a slight bow.

"This was the start of our journey, sir," Greg said. Removing the stele from his pocket he handed it to D'Trelna. Borrowed from Bob, then forgotten in the excitement, it had been there since the Clam Shack.

"What do you call this language?" the XO asked, removing his translator to hear the intonation.

"Egyptian."

Smiling, he nodded and replaced his earpiece. "We call it I'Gopta. It was a colonial language of the Empire—one of a family of hieroglyphic languages used to reestablish the tools of written communication among lost colonies sunken to barbarism.''

Handing it back, he asked, "How did you come by it?''

Succinctly as possible, Zahava, John and Greg told the story. The K'Ronarin officers listened attentively, interrupting only to ask sharp, precise questions. When the Terrans had finished, the food was cold and the cups empty.

L'Wrona collected the plates, dumping them down a disposer. "Sounds like you stumbled onto an at least partially functioning Imperial base," he said, resuming his seat. "Maybe even a full Colonial Service planetary installation with defenses intact.

"Which," he added thoughtfully, "would explain why a S'Cotar garrison isn't now nestled among your rotting corpses.''

"But it wasn't a very large place, just a few rooms," protested Zahava.

"Oh, it need not have been," said D'Trelna. "If there is a transport system, it would girdle the planet. You could have been in just one station. We may assume the computer's functioning, judging from the way you were forced into the transporter web.''

"Just before your arrival," L'Wrona said, "a S'Cotar assault unit teleported aboard from a satellite base orbiting the fourth planet. They and their base were destroyed, but not before they got off a distress call. Enemy reinforcements could be here in as little as a day. It's vital that we land and remove whatever equipment we can.''

"Vital to whom?" John frowned. "If the only thing preventing the S'Cotar from slaughtering four billion Terrans is that system, you surely don't plan to tamper with it?''

The Captain looked him in the eye. "I hope it isn't a question of choosing which of our peoples is to survive," he said carefully. "I've already sent for reinforcements, but the S'Cotar fleet is much closer than our own. If we can recover the nexus of a transport system, my duty is to take it at once to a Confederation base. We've already lost some fifteen billion people behind that red veil, and each day the S'Cotar press their attacks more boldly. Without that transporter, we fall.

And then the day that ancient computer on your planet fails, or the S'Cotar find a way to defeat it, your billions will join ours in death.

"In tactics and initiative, we're superior," he continued. "With the transporter, we can nullify the advantage the S'Cotar's teleportation abilities give them. We'll crush them.

"I hope the price of their defeat won't be another planet— yours. But if it is, so be it. I'll sacrifice Terra as readily as I would a K'Ronarin world."

D'Trelna rose. "Commander L'Wrona will show you to your quarters. Get some rest. We'll be landing in six hours."

Before the Terrans could speak, the Captain was gone and L'Wrona was ushering them down the corridor.

CHAPTER 8

D'TRELNA WAS SURE he'd just closed his eyes when K'Raoda signaled. "Captain, we're now orbiting the third planet."

Groaning, he rolled over and pressed a wall switch. "It's called Terra," he grunted. "Place us in synchronous orbit over our guests' point of origin and ask them to the bridge. I'll be right there. And wake L'Wrona up," he added maliciously, rolling to his feet.

"But sir, he just went to his cabin."

"Thin people don't need as much sleep, Subcommander," said D'Trelna, sitting up. "Get him up."

"We'll set you down with the landing party," he said to the Terrans a few moments later. The bags under their eyes told of a sleepless offwatch. In their boots, you'd be a bit upside down, too, he thought. "I'd appreciate your showing Subcommander K'Raoda the site and acting as liaison when local authorities arrive."

"You anticipate detection?" asked John.

The Captain nodded. "*Implacable*'s shielded, but the shuttle's not. It will knife past your air defenses before a single fighter can be launched. But I'm sure its landing point will be quickly found." He smiled. "I'd like to be in your defense headquarters for the next few hours, watching the fun.

"Good luck. K'Raoda, if you need—"

He was interrupted by a cry of "Enemy contact!"

"Report," ordered D'Trelna, whirling to face L'Wrona.

"Three vessels," the XO responded, slender fingers playing over his console, eyes scanning the readout. "Just came out of hyperdrive almost exactly where we did. At present course and speed, about five hours to contact.''

"Can you make out their type?" asked the Captain, sinking into the command chair.

"Running an analysis now." Then: "Three heavy cruisers of the new 'Berserker' class."

D'Trelna ignored K'Raoda's astonished whistle.

"They've undoubtedly detected us," said L'Wrona, turning from the screen. "S'Cotar cruisers have gear as good as our own."

"We can't outfight three heavy cruisers, Captain," K'Raoda said, walking toward his station. He left four very worried Terrans standing by the door. "Shall we prepare for hyperspace?"

"You run, Captain," said John, grim-faced, "and you'll leave four billion humans defenseless before those "

D'Trelna jabbed a blunt finger at the angry Terran.

"Don't tell me my duty!" he snapped. "I commanded *Dauntless* at T'Qar—a relic against a S'Cotar flotilla. I lost two hundred good men, but we bought time for an evacuation convoy.

"You are, however, correct," he said in a softer tone, temper recovered. "I can't run. Not without knowing if those hypothetical Imperial defenses would protect you from a very real enemy. We stand."

"Captain, three heavy cruisers?" L'Wrona said, quietly seconding K'Raoda's protest.

"We will fight and we will win, gentlemen," said D'Trelna confidently, nodding. He turned to the Terrans. "As for you people, please stay with the landing force until our return. They'll need your help even more now. I can't spare many men.

"K'Raoda." He fixed the young officer with a piercing gaze. "If you are in imminent danger of being overrun by a S'Cotar assault force, destroy as much of that installation as you can. You're authorized to arm these and any other Terrans at your discretion."

"Sir, what about the Non-Interference Directive?" asked the Tactics Officer.

"A pleasant fiction whose time has passed."

"You'll be staying here for now?" he asked, turning to McShane. Better, though still a bit pale, the professor sat at the flag station.

He nodded. "I'd be of little use in a ground action right now."

Accompanying the landing party to the now-restored Hangar Deck, Bob warmly embraced Zahava and Greg as they boarded the stubby-winged shuttle.

"You know what your chances are," said John, lingering.

Bob nodded. "About as good as yours if those S'Cotar cruisers get through. Besides"—he grinned—"I'll go out astride the deck of a starship, battling alien hordes. Beats the hell out of a coronary."

Ten minutes later, as McShane followed his commando escort back into the ship, the battle klaxon sounded.

The small ship settled with a quiet *whoosh* atop Goose Hill. Fighting back waves of nausea, John managed to croak, "Do you always pilot like that, Subcommander? Or just when you have guests?" He knew all of his bones were broken.

Seemingly untouched by the g-forces, the K'Ronarin officer bounded past his passengers to the airlock. Deftly fingering a control panel, he opened both doors. Fresh sea air wafted in.

"If you'd seen the sensors," he said as his squad fanned out, securing the perimeter, "you'd have dived, too. Your atmosphere is one vast detector web. We've no shield to stop missiles—I'd rather outrun them *before* they're fired."

Dropping like a meteor through the stratosphere, they'd executed a series of punishing, powered turns. Pressed deep into his padded chair by the brutal pressure, John had watched, gasping for air, as they'd plummeted through the clouds. Cobalt-blue, the Atlantic had rushed up, filling the overhead screen. Only at the last possible instant had a ribbon of dun-colored land appeared, curving out into the water. The shuttle's gentle landing had belied its violent descent.

John staggered to his feet. "I thought these warsuits doubled as pressure suits?" he said accusatively. "I blacked out more than once." He and Zahava helped an ashen-cheeked Greg to his feet.

"Without them, you'd be dead—we all would," said K'Raoda, turning in the airlock. "But they are better warsuits than pressure suits. Not even the Imperials could mutate so many physical laws with one construct.

"Come help us unload the cargo bay. You'll feel better."

They began moving supplies and equipment from the shuttle. Rubble still blocked the site's top entrance, but there was no sign of Langston or his men.

Leaving only two crewmen on guard, the small party of humans worked quickly, trucking cargo down to the hill's shoulder and stacking it before the rock-choked doorway. They finished as the sun was slipping into the ocean, turning the calm sea a burnt-ochre.

"Now what?" asked Zahava, eyeing the rubble.

K'Raoda sighed. "Give them the rifles, D'Nir."

Nodding, the NCO walked to a rectangular box, sliding back the top. The rifles he handed the Terrans were a gray, dully burnished metal. Stock, trigger guard, safety catch—all looked the same as on any rifle the three had held before. Only the lack of a protruding magazine and the odd muzzle gave the weapons an alien look.

"This will probably get me court-martialed," K'Raoda said resignedly, picking up a rifle. His men stood behind him in a small knot, watching the lesson.

"This is a Confederation Fleet Commando Ion-Laser Rifle, Model-Thirty-Two. It's a line-of-sight weapon, firing a stream of ions along a laser beam. The M-Thirty-Two has greater range and power than the M-Eleven pistol." He patted his holster. "It doesn't require any gift of intellect to use one. Just point"—he aimed casually into the rubble—"and fire." A boulder exploded with a bang, pierced by a thin, red bolt. The blaster made a distinctive shrilling when fired.

"Adjust the beam so." He twisted the muzzle, then fired again. The beam fanned wide, slowly melting an entire boulder.

"Please," K'Raoda implored, tossing his rifle to D'Nir, "keep the safety on.

"One more thing. Recall that the S'Cotar can appear human. If your communicator"—he touched the pendant at his throat—"sounds like this . . ." A high-pitched whine made them wince. ". . . then there's a S'Cotar within twenty yards. Shoot whomever you think you see without hesitation—your mother, your lover, your child—and you may live. Understood?"

His students nodded.

"Good." He smiled. "Now for some target practice. Help us blast through the rubble. I want to be safely inside by dark."

The tons of rubble soon melted away under the hungry red beams. With everyone lending a hand, they made K'Raoda's deadline.

CHAPTER 9

BILL SUTHERLAND SMILED at the young, blond-headed guard. "Do you know what a John Doe warrant is?" he asked, leaning against the big security desk.

The man shook his head, eyes narrowed in suspicion. There was a stubborn set to his mouth.

"It's issued by a federal judge who agrees with me that some of Leurre's staff conspired to kill one of my men," he continued easily. "We're empowered to arrest anyone we believe part of that conspiracy. You're obstructing our investigation, which makes you an accessory after the fact and subject to arrest. Understand?"

"Yeah." A corner of his mouth curled up—more grimace than smile.

"So why not cooperate? It'll save FBI Special Agent Flannigan here"—he nodded to his right—"from having to haul you in." Tall, thirtyish, black Irish good looks, Flannigan stood with Tuckman, Bakunin and Sutherland's team in the deserted lobby of the Leurre Institute. The guard was the only other human being they'd seen since their arrival.

Sullenly answering Bill's questions, he'd given nothing away. No, he didn't know where Dr. Langston was. No, there was no one here today. Yes, the Institute was usually open on Friday. No, he would not look at their search warrant. They'd have to wait till he could locate someone in authority.

Bill's soft persuasion seemed to work. "Okay"—the guard shrugged—"if you have to search, search. There's nothing I can do. But there really isn't anyone here. And I don't know where the Director is."

Sutherland turned to his men. "Okay, let's get started. You all know where to go and what to look for. Remember, we don't have to uncover the whole iceberg—the tip will do for now. Anything on Foxfire, Antonucchi's murder, the Goose Hill site. Then tomorrow we can have fifty men down here, sifting through.

"You've all got handsets." He held up his own small, Japanese-made transceiver. "If you find something, let us know. I'll be here with the DCI and Colonel Bakunin, in case any of the staff show up."

"Why weren't your people at Otis, Bill?" asked the Director as the agents boarded an elevator.

His deputy shook his head. "I wish I knew. Perhaps Langston caught up with them—an unpleasant possibility. Or maybe they went back to the site." His face brightened. "Of course, that's just what they'd do! McShane would want to poke around in there before we sealed it off."

Tuckman nodded. "Good reasoning. Let's finish our preliminaries here, then get to the site." Turning to the guard, he asked, "How do we get to Goose Hill from here?"

"It'd be easier if I drew you a map." The man opened a drawer as Tuckman turned back to Sutherland.

"This reminds me of an operation we ran in Vienna after the war," he said. "We didn't know—"

Impaled on a brilliant shaft of purest indigo, Tuckman stood for a surprised instant, then fell to the floor, his chest a charred, smoking ruin. A high-pitched whine pierced the air. Whirling, the guard turned his strange weapon toward Sutherland, then slid from sight beneath the big teak desk. A faint pop heralded his disappearance.

Bakunin holstered his slim, silenced Italian automatic. "Training pays," he said calmly.

Dazed and pale, Sutherland closed Tuckman's dead, staring eyes, then walked to the security station, retrieving the strange, long-barreled pistol from the desk top. Doing so, he caught sight of the guard's body.

"Bakunin," he croaked, gesturing. The Russian followed him behind the desk. They stood together, looking down at the dead six-foot insectoid: deep-green, bulbous-eyed, it faintly resembled a huge praying mantis, except for the tentacles tapering from its two upper limbs—tentacles still twitching in death shock. A webbed belt, hung with unfamiliar equipment, girdled its thorax. A viscous green liquid oozed from a neat hole between the eyes.

Standing there over the dead alien, the stench of Tuckman's burnt flesh filling the room, the small, high moments of Bill Sutherland's life touched his mind. The clapboard Indiana farmhouse, acres of white unfurled behind it on wash day. Dad, Grandpa and the uncles playing around the cribbage board on Christmas Eve, sipping bourbon, the air heavy with blue cigar smoke. Lois's encircling warmth that first time in the back of his old Chevy, under a full August moon, the air rich with the scent of wild roses. Inge's startling blue eyes, that day in Berlin. Emmy-chan in the snow at Nikko, and much, much later, lying before their fireplace in McLean, the firelight dancing along her soft, golden skin.

It all felt very fragile now.

"Bakunin," he said softly, "I think we've found a little green gremlin." Unnoticed, his hands shook.

Bakunin finally found his voice. It quivered. "It is alien, intelligent, hostile and armed with superior weaponry, Sutherland. It seems capable of some form of mind control. I urge you to summon reinforcements. Cordon off the village."

His hand still shaking, Sutherland picked up the phone, punching out a long series of digits.

Major General James ("Big Jim") O'Brien's twenty-five years in the air force had added only slightly to his bedrock of Missouri skepticism. Thus he blinked twice at the situation board before startling the noncom next to him with a loud, "What the hell is that?"

"That," to the thirty pairs of eyes in the Joint Chiefs of Staff Operations center, four hundred feet under the Pentagon, was a green dot moving fast—much too fast—across the North Atlantic toward the New England coast. As they watched, the computer tagged it "U1": unidentified target, number one. Not yet "H" for hostile, just "U." That "U" worried Big Jim far more than an "H." "H" he knew how to deal with.

"Sure it's not a Russian?" he asked hopefully.

"No way, sir," said the Target ID officer, staring at his CRT. "Too fast, too high. It originated in space, outside our radar range. If it were Russian, we'd have picked up launch."

"Meteor?"

"It's changed trajectory eight times in the past minute and is now decelerating. Not to any speed we could intercept, though." The Sergeant avoided the General's eyes. Before O'Brien could speak, the green dot entered U.S. territory and disappeared. "Wet landing?" he demanded.

"No, General. Probably land. Just. A stretch of coast along Cape Cod. There." He typed quickly into his terminal. A red "X" now flashed a third of the way up the peninsula, itself enlarged on the situation board.

Shit, thought O'Brien desperately. A goddamned UFO on my watch. And the mother's landed. He squeezed his eyes shut for an instant, then opened them. The red cross was still there, blinking now.

O'Brien picked up the green phone. In seconds he was listening to the Otis Operations Officer's cool, crisp report. Yes, their radar had spotted it, too. A squadron of F-15s had scrambled.

Glancing at the board, O'Brien saw a phalanx of red crosses, marked F1–F5, appear, cruising along the Cape's Atlantic shore. "Get some choppers up, too, Major Jenkins," he ordered. "If you've had no luck by dawn we'll reinforce you."

As he hung up the green phone, the blue one next to it rang: three brisk chimes, like a ship's clock. Everyone who could turned to watch as O'Brien reached for it. The blue phone never rang.

"General O'Brien," he answered. It was going to be a night.

"General," said a crisp voice, "this is William Sutherland, CIA. I'm declaring Situation Breakout. You'll find the applicable challenge and countersign in your standing orders. Please key to that program. This is not a drill."

O'Brien dutifully pecked "Breakout" on his terminal. "'Cortez,'" he read off the screen.

"*Gotterdämmerung*," responded Sutherland, hoping to God

he'd given the right countersign. There were only ten he had to memorize, but they changed every month. He was relieved to hear the General ask, "What are your instructions, Mr. Sutherland?"

"I need infantry at Oystertown, Massachusetts—the Leurre Oceanographic Institute. Get me some help as fast as you can from Otis—APs, air commandos, anyone who can carry a weapon. Things are a bit dicey here.

"Then get a Rapid Deployment Strike Force to Otis and quarantine Cape Cod. Maximum air vigilance in this sector.

"I'm calling the White House now, requesting Red Alert/Defense Condition Four. I'm authorized to instruct you to go to Yellow/DEFCON Three. Please do so now. I'll wait."

Mad dogs and the CIA, O'Brien thought, turning to his second in command. "Bradshaw," he said, "go to Yellow."

The Colonel looked up, startled, at the big board. Except for Cape Cod, all was normal.

"General?" he asked.

"Yellow, please, Colonel," O'Brien repeated firmly. "Per contingency."

"Very good, sir," said Bradshaw. Turning back to his console, he began issuing the necessary orders.

"Okay, Sutherland," the General said, "you've got thirty minutes to get me White House confirmation of this alert, or we stand down. You know the drill."

"I know the drill."

"You realize this will put the world on a war footing?" added O'Brien. The command center was now bustling with activity as the alert went out and acknowledgments poured in.

Sutherland glanced down at the dead alien. "I certainly hope so, General."

"Be advised," said O'Brien, "that there is a stratospheric craft of advanced design and unknown origin operating in your vicinity. It's probably landed. Otis is up looking for it now."

"What do you mean, 'advanced'?" demanded the CIA officer.

"I mean, Sutherland," O'Brien tersely replied, voice lowered, "that we're von Richthofen's circus and it's an F-Fifteen."

"Give me your number. I'll call you with your reinforcements' ETA." He took it and hung up.

"What was all that Wagnerian gibberish?" asked Bakunin.

"'*Gotterdämmerung*'?" Sutherland smiled thinly. "A contingency established shortly after Foxfire began, I now note.

"The phrase 'extraterrestrial invasion' is never used, but the plan calls for area quarantine, full alert and even projects nuking our own cities to stop an 'enemy' landing. I never really believed it was meant just to stop some Ukrainian paratroopers."

They turned at the slight rumble of an elevator door opening. Flannigan stood alone in the elevator, dazed, unmoving, pistol held limply in one hand. The door started to close.

"Flannigan!" snapped Sutherland. At that, the FBI agent's hand shot out, banging back the door. He stepped out, blinking, seeming to see Bakunin and Sutherland for the first time.

"Lab worker in marine biology tried to shoot me," he said slowly, walking to the desk. "I shot first, then she, it—" He stopped short, spotting Tuckman's head protruding from behind the security station. "What happened?" he asked hoarsely.

"First, holster your weapon," ordered Sutherland. Flannigan complied, slipping his revolver into the holster nestled under his left arm. "Now look behind the desk. Was that what you killed?"

Flannigan peered down over the desk top. Biting his lower lip, he nodded. "It killed the DCI," he surmised, looking up.

Bill nodded. "Never knew what hit him. And neither do we," he added, hefting the dead alien's weapon.

"I'll recall the others, Tim." He placed a gentle hand on the younger man's shoulder. "Get yourself some coffee. There are some vending machines down that hall, on the left." He pointed to where a corridor curved out of sight across the lobby, opposite the elevators. "I'll call you."

The agent had gone perhaps ten yards when Bill called casually, "Oh, Tim. When did you become right-handed?"

Flannigan whirled, hand flashing toward his pistol even as Bakunin reached for his own gun and Sutherland fired. A bright-blue bolt took the agent full in the face. His form shimmering, he fell like a stone.

Two dead insectoids now lay in the Institute's lobby, their deep-hued green a stark contrast to the floor's blue-veined Florentine marble.

"You know, Sutherland," said Bakunin, putting his pistol away, "we—you and me—are the only ones here we *know* aren't . . . those." He nodded at Flannigan's killer, its short, thin neck ending in a charred stump. "The safest thing, I regret to say, would be to shoot your men as they get off the elevator." He stopped at the American's hard stare.

"*Tovarich* Colonel Bakunin," said Sutherland coldly, "you are a ruthless son of a bitch. If Marsh, Johnson and Yazanaga aren't Marsh, Johnson and Yazanaga, I'll know. But until I know, all are innocent."

The KGB officer shrugged. "You're a sentimental fool, Sutherland," he said. "And as for ruthless, which of us just spoke of nuking his own country?"

"Did it occur to you, Bakunin, that Flannigan might have been a gremlin all along?" Before the Russian could answer, Bill picked up his radio and recalled his men. Receiving the last acknowledgment, he turned to the phone, then paused. "Why did they jump us, Bakunin? They could easily have carried off the masquerade."

"Perhaps," he said slowly, "they thought we knew more than we did. Or maybe something is happening elsewhere that we're unaware of, Sutherland. I mean, where are they all?" He looked around the deserted lobby. "They should have swarmed over us."

Picking up the phone again, the CIA officer dialed out. "They knew, Bakunin. They knew they were blown! But not by us. It all must tie into the site and my missing people. As soon as I make this call . . .

"Yes, José Montanoya, please. William Sutherland, CIA. Find him. This is a national emergency."

CHAPTER 10

McSHANE WAS ENJOYING the hospitality of *Implacable*'s bridge. He'd just polished off a plateful of tasty, unfamiliar food when L'Wrona called, "We'll be within range in four hours, Captain." The XO sat at the Tactics station vacated by K'Raoda. "No change in enemy status."

"Engagement point?" D'Trelna eyed the three S'Cotar ships' position, shown relative to *Implacable*'s on the central screen.

"Midpoint between the asteroid belt and the fourth planet."

L'Wrona turned to McShane. "Did you know that asteroid belt was once a planet, destroyed artificially?"

Bob started. "How can you tell?"

"Radiation traces common to the whole belt. Someone dropped a planetbuster on it a few million years ago. Planetbusters have very long half-lives."

"Stand by for hyperspace," the Captain ordered. Turning away from the screen, he met his men's startled looks.

"Sir, I thought we were going to fight," said L'Wrona after an instant's hesitation.

"Oh, we are," D'Trelna replied. "But we're no match for three heavy cruisers, even with our hodgepodge of Imperial systems."

He smiled at their confusion. "Our drive, though, because it is Imperial, allows for short, very precise jumps. We're going to drop right into that task force."

"Sir, the drive has never been tested to those tolerances," protested N'Trol. He took a step away from his station. "Anything could go wrong."

"Archives assures us that the Imperials ran their drives to such close tolerances," replied the Captain easily.

"But sir, that was thousands of years ago!"

"Bah! You overhauled that equipment yourself, Commander, no more than six months ago. You're the best engineer in the Confederation, N'Trol. That drive will perform as specified, I have no doubt." D'Trelna waved down any further protests.

"I'm warmed by your respect for my command ability," he said gravely. "Now shall wc stand by for hyperspace?"

They had jumped to it, L'Wrona running figures and laying in coordinates, the rest busying themselves at their stations. An alert klaxon hooted.

"Cycling up, Captain. Two minutes eight seconds to jump." The XO's tone was one of quiet efficiency.

"Quite a little democracy you have here, Captain," Bob observed amid the bustle.

"We've been an independent rabble for a long time, Professor." D'Trelna smiled crookedly, half-turning toward the Terran. "A trait, happily, not yet undone by the present emergency.

"There are some"—his face clouded—"who'd like to see a return to the grand ways of the Imperium. The glory of battle, the unthinking obedience, the stifling of initiative. And perhaps, if this war continues much longer, they'll have their way." Lips pursed, he nodded thoughtfully, then stabbed a finger at the deck. "But not on my ship," he growled.

"How long is the jump?" McShane asked after a moment.

"Ten nanoseconds," said L'Wrona, picking up on the question.

"Please tell our guest what an error of a picosecond would do," D'Trelna said. "I want him to appreciate my daring."

The XO nodded, looking up from his console, his work finished. He swiveled to meet McShane's gaze. "One picosecond short will cause us to blow up, far from our target. One picosecond over and we'll explode inside the sixth planet."

"An event that wouldn't do us or the planet much good," D'Trelna observed dryly.

L'Wrona glanced back at his console. "One minute to jump."

"Set all Weapons systems to automatic, Mr. N'Dreyna," the Captain ordered the Weapons Officer, "and tie them in with Tactics' program."

"All systems tied in, sir," the young Ensign reported.

"Should I strap myself in, or something?" Bob asked, hands searching his chair for belt or harness. There wasn't any.

"Don't worry." The XO leaned back in his chair, eyes on the screen. "It will be over before our minds can comprehend—one way or the other.

"Thirty seconds."

"If we're very lucky," the Captain said to no one in particular, "their shields will be down, so far from Terra. We'll emerge from nowhere and blow them away."

"Fifteen seconds."

"Of course," he mused, "if not . . ."

"Ten seconds."

"Their shields will be up . . ."

"Five seconds."

"And they'll blast *us*."

"Jump!"

McShane thought his stomach flopped, but later wrote it off to imagination. There seemed to be no transition. One instant they were alone in space, the next the screen blazed with light. It was over before Bob could blink.

"All targets destroyed!" The usually reserved L'Wrona leaped up, pounding his smirking Captain on the back. *Implacable* reverberated to jubilant whoops and the screech of alarms touched off in celebration.

Good-naturedly enduring the tumult for a moment, D'Trelna finally held up his hands. "All right, everyone! Stations, please!

"We were damn lucky," he said as the din subsided. "But our mission's far from accomplished. We have to return to Terra and our men."

"How long to return?" asked McShane as the bridge sank back into routine.

"Six hours," said D'Trelna. "I'm not about to risk that little maneuver again. Insincere assurances to Commander N'Trol notwithstanding.

"Let us hope the landing party is all right."

Innocent of danger, the tow-headed boy bounded up the path, into Zahava's blaster sights. Communicator shrilling in her ear, she swallowed hard and pressed the trigger.

Dying, the boy-form shimmered into what the Israeli recognized as a S'Cotar warrior. "The bugs are attacking," she called over the tactical circuit.

Helmetless, the pilot she'd been guarding raced out of the shuttle, rifle in hand. And died, lanced through the head by a blaster bolt from the rocks below.

Zahava threw herself behind one of the shuttle's thick landing struts, her helmet's infrared scanners picking out the ochre blotches of S'Cotar massing along the hill's lee. Throwing the rifle to her shoulder, she poured a withering series of quick bursts into the insectoids. A hundred blue bolts flashed back at her, filling the night sky.

"Zahava! Hold on! We're coming!" John's voice roared over the commnet.

He was there in less than a minute, Greg and one of K'Raoda's men zigzagging up behind him. Heavy S'Cotar fire now bracketed the Israeli's position.

"Can these suits take simultaneous hits?" John asked the K'Ronarin. He ducked instinctively as a bolt tore through the strut, showering them with sparks. He glanced warily at the tons of spacecraft perched above their heads as the crewman replied. "Only for a few seconds. It depends on how heavy the fire is." The man, a middle-aged Communications technician, sighted carefully and fired. A distant boulder flared cherry-red as a form scuttled from behind it. The K'Ronarin cut it down with a negligent wave of his hand blaster.

A fusillade of blaster fire riddled the shuttle, tearing great gashes in the hull.

"The fuel cells will go!" cried the K'Ronarin. Hastily, the four humans low-crawled to the cover of the rocks behind them.

The craft went up with a roar, sending a huge pillar of blue flame shooting skyward. Molten debris rained down, sparking scores of small brush fires, through which the S'Cotar advanced.

"K'Raoda, we can't hold here," John called over the tactical band. "They've blown the shuttle and are advancing in strength. What's your status?"

"They're coming up our side of the hill. Hundreds of them. I've lost two men." The young officer's voice mingled with the crackle and whine of blaster fire. "We're falling back to the tunnel, Harrison. Join us."

John covered as the others withdrew. No matter how many insectoids he mowed down, more swarmed up from the beach, firing as they came. Soon his warsuit started taking multiple hits, forcing him to withdraw. He followed the others at a run, stopping only twice to snap off a few shots.

So intense was the return fire that for the last few yards John's warsuit was encased in a rippling aura of raw energy. He dived behind the temporary shelter of a boulder, joining the surviving humans now huddled among the rocks ringing the site's entrance.

A stunning barrage of light and sound swept over their shelter, shattering rock and shaking the earth.

"Fall back!" K'Raoda shouted above the din.

They charged into the tunnel, securing the door a second before another, stronger barrage rocked their previous position.

"Photon mortars!" exclaimed K'Raoda. Leaning against the wall, he checked his blaster charge. "Either they've landed a task force or there's a Nest on this planet."

Zahava was about to ask what a Nest was when Greg asked, "Can they get through this door?"

"Yes," said *Implacable*'s Tactics Officer. "But it'll take a while. It only looks like rock. Actually, it's a derivative of Imperial battlesteel." He tapped the door with his gun butt. "Nothing tougher."

"Well I know," the geologist said with a wry smile.

"Why don't they just teleport in here, K'Raoda?" asked John.

"Either they don't have the coordinates or are afraid we've laid some nasty surprises for them."

"My God! Where'd they all come from?" The Israeli slumped wearily against the wall. "We littered the ground with them, but still they kept coming."

"From what you told us," said K'Raoda, "the nearby oceanographic institute must be their Nest. They probably quietly killed off the staff and were using it to search for this site."

"Cindy!" Greg's eyes widened in alarm. "She's at the Institute."

"Who's 'Cindy'?" K'Raoda demanded sharply.

John explained.

The K'Ronarin officer grasped Greg by the shoulders. "Answer carefully," he said intently. "How long did you know her?"

Blinking, the Terran met his gaze. "Three months."

"Lived with her?"

"Yes."

"How long?"

"About a month."

K'Raoda nodded, then pressed on. "Did you ever notice anything unusual about Cindy? Inappropriate mannerisms, dress, speech?"

Greg shook his head, mute.

"I only saw her once," John said. "She was dressed very lightly for a raw, rainy day. She looked comfortable."

"Just as Langston bounded up Goose Hill with no sign of exertion!" exclaimed Zahava.

The K'Ronarin turned back to Greg. "Do you have any vivid memories of sex with her," he asked bluntly, "or just an indistinct recollection of a wonderful, glowing experience?"

Greg frowned. "I . . . I can't recall anything." He shook his head, bemused. "I remember clearly every other woman I've ever had—but not her."

K'Raoda released the geologist. "That's because there was no 'her,' my friend. 'Cindy' was a S'Cotar. If ever such a woman existed, she's long dead."

"That would explain how Langston—how the S'Cotar—knew we were on the hill," said Zahava. "And that nice, freckle-faced girl I slept under the same roof with—". She broke off, eyes widening in horror.

"Was a transmute that could have ripped your throat out," said K'Raoda.

"But why?" Greg's voice was anguished. "Why lure me back to Massachusetts, why ask to marry me?"

"You were the last human who knew where this site was," John guessed. "To kill you outright would have drawn even more unwelcome attention to the Institute. Better a wedding in Louisiana and a tragic honeymoon accident."

Greg went to a corner, squatted and noisily threw up, rocking back and forth on his heels. Standing after a moment, he shook off comforting hands and confronted his friends, face pale and grim. "What now?" he demanded.

"We hold until relieved, or until I can awaken this installation's slumbering guardian," said K'Raoda. He turned to Zahava. "Show me the control room you were shanghaied from. I'll try to activate the ground defenses. Unless *Implacable* returns soon, that's our only chance.

"We'll make our last stand at the control room, then destroy it.

"Hold as long as you can," he called over his shoulder, following Zahava down the stairs. "Make them pay for every inch."

"We'll redo the floors in vulture-vomit-green," John promised, turning to face the door. It'd begun to glow just a bit under the hellish energies clawing at it out of the night.

CHAPTER 11

BILL SUTHERLAND LED his small contingent along the cold
dark beach, stumbling now and again over frozen clumps of
seaweed. The bitter March wind howled off the Atlantic, driving the frigid evening tide at their feet.

Bill wasn't aware of his numb hands or frozen feet. With the
others, his whole attention was held by Goose Hill, its summit
now lit by the flash of massed energy weapons, their whining
clear above wind and surf.

Even as he watched, a huge explosion tore open the night,
throwing him and his men to the sand, bathing them in an
ochre glow.

"Sweet Jesus." He stumbled to his feet, squinting into the
glare. S'Cotar warriors swarmed unopposed past the fiercely
burning shuttle.

"Someone friendly to us is up there, and in big trouble!"
Bakunin's shout carried over the secondary explosions. Like
the rest, he'd traded his business suit for more practical
clothing from the Institute: turtleneck wool sweater, heavy
twill pants and a fur-lined field jacket, the Leurre Institute
dolphin crest on its left shoulder. And like the Americans, he
carried an M-16, also "borrowed" from the Institute.

"Sure looks that way." Sutherland nodded, dropping his
voice as the explosions died. "How do we get to them,
though?" He pointed his rifle up at the carnage. "We can't
fight our way through *that*!"

The small pickup force from Otis—APs, mechanics, pro-
grammers—had secured the Institute. The infantry brigade,

though, was still forming up at Ft. Devens. Before leaving Oystertown, Bill had changed half the airmobile brigade's destination from the Institute to Goose Hill, but it would be at least another hour before their arrival. Whoever was holding the hill didn't have an hour.

Suddenly it came to Bill. He knew how to bypass the summit.

"There's a tunnel leading from the site here to the beach," he said, sweeping his light along the embankment as they walked. "My people escaped through it and one of them left his stick as a guide. If we're lucky, it'll still be there."

Yazanaga spotted it, just as more explosions rocked the ground: a blackthorn walker leaning precariously against a great boulder. As they approached at a trot, the ground shook again and the stick fell with a clatter, rolling to a stop at their feet.

Picking up the stick, Bakunin skeptically eyed the weathered granite. "So?"

"So . . . this!" With the air of a conjurer, Sutherland flashed his light into a small niche above where the stick had leaned. A tiny green light winked back as a great stone slab swung noiselessly aside.

The agents stood blinking in the yellow circle of light from the tunnel. Johnson gave a low whistle of astonishment.

Another barrage rocked the hill, sending a shower of loose rock down on their heads.

"Don't you believe it." Bill clicked his M-16's safety off. "My instincts tell me this is only the end of the beginning, as the man said."

"The same instincts that got us lost for two days in the sewers under the sixteenth aggrandizement, no doubt."

If Sutherland heard the crack, delivered *sotto voce*, he ignored it. "After you, *Tovarich* Colonel," he said, gesturing toward the entrance.

The Russian shook his head. "Your tunnel, you lead."

Rifle leveled, Bill stepped warily into the passage. Marsh, Yazanaga and Johnson, veteran cold warriors all, followed, weapons poised. Bakunin, bringing up the rear, covered the doorway till the slab swung shut, then trotted after the Americans.

* * *

"Piece of junk!" K'Raoda said through clenched teeth, glaring at the console's merrily twinkling lights. It was the first time Zahava had seen him lose his composure.

"All the positions were lit before," she said, staring at the other consoles, all dark.

"I think the last time you triggered the defenses," speculated the K'Ronarin. "Perhaps your metabolism is a bit different from ours. Or perhaps the computer has standing orders to transport intruders to the nearest manned station. Perhaps *Implacable* qualified. And perhaps I don't know what the hell I'm talking about," he concluded ruefully, returning to his task.

"According to the Imperial War Archives," he added, hopefully typing a fresh sequence of numbers, "the ground defenses can be activated from a remote terminal—assuming we're faced with a Mode Two or Three system. Anything higher and all bets are off." Zahava watched the screen respond to the input with a fresh burst of figures. Figures her brain knew, through the magic of the translator, to be mathematical symbols akin to calculus.

"Hmmm." K'Raoda stared hard at the new figures.

"Maybe?" asked the Israeli, peering eagerly over his shoulder.

"Maybe. I don't know." He rubbed his eyes. "What's worrying me is that the Planetary Operations Command series had a reputation for chattiness that's endured over fifty centuries. If this one were functioning, we shouldn't be able to shut it up."

They looked up, startled, as the shrill of blaster fire echoed down the tunnel.

"Cover the hall," ordered the officer, tapping again on the trilevel keyboard.

Rifle at high-port, Zahava ran from the room.

The outer door flared white, atomizing. Aiming carefully, the handful of humans fired into the packed S'Cotar, dimly visible through the haze and smoke. Harmless-looking, a small black ball rolled in.

The K'Ronarin commtech moved first.

"Grenade!" he cried, hurling himself atop the ball.

Even though his body absorbed much of the fearsome heat that vaporized it, his retreating comrades would have been broiled without their warsuits.

The commando Sergeant, D'Nir, leading, the survivors charged into the altar chamber and down the ladder into the lower tunnel. John, in the rear, secured the altar stone with a blast to the wall sensor. "That should hold 'em," he growled.

"Not for long," said the commando, running ahead of him. The small troop halted where Zahava waited, just outside the control room.

"Commander, I need a blastpack," D'Nir said, bursting in on K'Raoda.

"Over there." Not taking his eyes from the screen, the officer gestured toward their neat, small stack of equipment.

The Sergeant, no older than K'Raoda, ran to the pile. Tumbling it in his haste, he yanked out a flat gray packet, then charged back down the corridor.

K'Raoda typed in another sequence. "How long?" he asked over the commnet.

"Assuming maximum delay at the ladder—twenty minutes," D'Nir reported.

The NCO reappeared a moment later, sans blastpack. "It'll detonate when the first warrior reaches the bottom rung," he reported. "I set it only for that life form."

John poked his head through the doorway. "If you don't get that thing working soon," he said, "we're going to experience fatal overcrowding."

"If I do," replied K'Raoda, "the defenses may be inoperative. And if I don't—well, be grateful that we won't have to spend much longer in these dreary tunnels.

"Sergeant, plant nuclear demolition charges on this equipment. Set timers for command detonation and detonation within three feet of any nonhumanoid life form."

A dull *krump* punctuated his order. The floor shook as dust billowed in from the ruined altar well. Gagging and wheezing, the humans switched their warsuits to internal atmosphere.

It took only a moment, though, for the installation's scrubbers to sweep the air clean, affording a clear view of the first wave of S'Cotar as they rounded the tunnel, firing.

Crouching low, the defenders blasted back.

One crewman lost an arm to concentrated fire. His suit sealed the blood-gushing stump, clamping off the wound—but not before his agonized shrieks had filled the commnet.

The first wave of warriors, cut down, were followed by another. And another. And another, charging unwavering into the human blaster fire. The corridor became a charnel house, heaped high with dead S'Cotar.

John's blaster quit without warning. A quick look showed over half a charge left. Hearing curses, he looked up. All of their weapons had failed.

"Damper field!" spat D'Nir. "This is it." He drew a wicked-looking knife from his boot sheath.

"Their blasters won't work, will they?" asked Greg. He peered down the tunnel's curve, around which the S'Cotar had withdrawn.

"No." Leaning his useless rifle against the wall, the NCO took up position midtunnel. "It'll be small consolation, though. Form on me. Skirmish order."

The other commando and the three Terrans fell in beside him. "Commander!" he called. "Now or never."

"Never," said a resigned voice. Knife in hand, K'Raoda came to stand with his men.

John felt a hand squeeze his arm. Zahava stood next to him. "The French have a saying," she said with a sad smile. "*'Tout passe, tout casse, tout lasse.'* You know it?"

"Today's not our day to perish, my friend." He gave an answering squeeze, then let her hand fall away. "My bad knee doesn't hurt."

The warriors came at them six abreast, leaping toadlike over their dead, sweeping down on the humans, a great green flood. At twenty paces, John gamely fell into a fighting crouch. His left knee was throbbing.

"Drop!" roared a voice from behind. "Hit the deck!" The humans dropped, faces to the rock floor, as a hail of gunfire tore into the S'Cotar. The victorious charge became a rout.

Firing from the hip, Sutherland led his men after the retreating warriors. A final burst of fire killed the last of them just as they reached their blasters, stacked beside the altar well. The five men walked slowly back to where John and Zahava stood, helmets under their arms.

"Long night, Mr. Director?" John smiled weakly.

"Long night, Mr. Harrison." Bill nodded, smiling back. "In fact, I keep hoping I'll wake up soon."

"No chance. Thanks, Bill." He clapped his friend on the shoulder.

Zahava, ever direct, kissed Sutherland soundly on the lips.

"More. More." He grinned, tired but appreciative. She kissed him again.

"Something out of an opium dream," said Sutherland, nudging a torn S'Cotar corpse with his rifle butt.

"And who those people are, I'm afraid to ask," he said, nodding toward the K'Ronarin survivors. "I gather they supplied your galactic opera costumes?"

"They're from a nearby starship," said Greg nonchalantly, helping carry the unconscious crewman into the transport room. Sutherland merely nodded, eyes distant. Bakunin, standing nearby examining a blast rifle, didn't even look up.

"I can see you're overwhelmed by the news," drawled John.

"I was overwhelmed hours ago." The CIA officer sighed. "Now I'm just trying to cope, moment to moment. What are they called?"

"They're K'Ronarins," said Zahava. "Their ancestors built this installation, centuries ago."

"And the big green bugs?"

"S'Cotar. The two are fighting a war of extermination," John said.

"Who's winning?"

"The S'Cotar."

Sutherland grunted. "This gets cheerier by the minute."

K'Raoda had vanished into the transport room just after the warriors' destruction. Now he reappeared, intent on the small biosensor he was holding. After a moment he looked up, relieved. "All enemy forces have left the area." He gave a crooked grin. "We did it—we held.

"And it's because of you that we did," he said to Sutherland. "Thank you." He held out his hand.

"I can't understand you," said Bill, shaking hands, "but I can guess. You're welcome."

"By a clever oversight, I neglected to bring translators with us." K'Raoda led them into the transport room. Bakunin, exploring, looked up as they trooped in.

"May I present Colonel Andreyev Ivanovich Bakunin, Union of Soviet Socialist Republics," said Sutherland. "These two people"—he indicated John and Zahava—"work with me."

Bakunin nodded pleasantly. "May I know their names?"

"No." Bill looked at Greg. "You, I don't know," he said.

"If you're Joe Antonucchi's boss, you might recognize my fingerprints from a piece of granite I gave him."

"*Implacable* to ground force." D'Trelna's voice boomed from the commset and over all the communicators. "What is your situation?" A ragged cheer preceded K'Raoda's report.

"I'm coming down with reinforcements," the Captain said, an anxious McShane hovering at his elbow. "By the way, fifty Terran rotoplanes are closing on you—ETA two minutes. I assume they're friendly." (He assumed nothing. Four batteries were locked on the unsuspecting airborne troops.)

John relayed the information to Sutherland.

"RDF troops from Devens." He nodded. "I'd better get up there. Where's the front door?"

His men hadn't been idle. A rope ladder now dangled down the altar well. He made a face, then swung up the ladder, K'Raoda following close behind.

"I don't know about anyone else," said Bakunin, "but I need rest." The Russian lay down on the floor and was instantly asleep.

"Food for those who want it," said D'Nir, passing out handfuls of tasteless protein wafers.

Tired but hungry, the remaining allies ate.

CHAPTER 12

"YES, BUT WHY didn't they teleport?"

D'Trelna's bull voice filled the cramped transport room. "You should all be dead!" He'd landed an hour ago, marched in and promptly taken command. Unlike K'Raoda, he'd brought extra translators.

Rumpled green tunic unbuttoned, the Captain perched precariously atop one of the slender console chairs, drumming his fingers on the instrument panel. "Too many unanswered questions, gentlemen," he said to the K'Ronarins and Terrans gathered around him. He enumerated them on his blunt fingers.

"One. The S'Cotar have been in your solar system for some time. That's obvious from the base we destroyed, their takeover of the oceanographic facility and their destruction, according to your own evidence, of other transporter stations.

"Two." A second finger rose. "Given all that, you people"—he nodded toward the Terrans—"have no more right to be alive than my landing party. The S'Cotar should have swept through you like voracious insects devouring a grainfield. Just as they should have devoured this planet years ago. Why didn't they?

"And three." A thumb came up. "They should have teleported down that tunnel once they were through the outer door and could visualize the area. Hell! They should have overrun you on the hilltop. Why didn't they use the ability that has cost us so dearly—an ability that threatens to sweep us from the galaxy?"

He slapped the dull black metal on the console. "Bah! I'm

not an Alienpsych officer. Let's keep those points in mind, though, and get on to the specifics of staying alive. Questions?''

"Are we in any immediate danger of attack?" asked Sutherland. He'd exchanged the S'Cotar blaster for a K'Ronarin rifle, now slung over his shoulder. Marsh, Johnson, Yazanaga and Bakunin were also toting Fleet M-32s.

"Tactics Officer?" D'Trelna deferred to K'Raoda.

"Almost certainly," answered the younger man, his work at the terminal momentarily set aside. "The S'Cotar invariably counterattack. We've been granted this brief lull, I suspect, so they can rally everything they've got left in your system—spacecraft, transmutes, warriors—and launch a coordinated assault. Right now they're probably marshaling on the opposite side of the planet from *Implacable*. The festivities should resume soon, I think."

"How long before your fleet gets here?" asked McShane.

"A week, maybe two." D'Trelna held up a hand, stifling the murmur of dismay. "Not soon enough to help us, obviously. But soon enough, I hope, to take care of major S'Cotar reinforcements. If we can hold till then, we may win. If not . . ."

"How can we help?" asked Bakunin. "More troops?"

("Pretty free with our men, isn't he?" someone   Marsh?—stage-whispered.)

"No." D'Trelna shook his head. "In fact, you should withdraw all but a small number of men—say forty. If we can't hold these few tunnels with a hundred men, we can't hold them at all. Don't forget, the S'Cotar have a fix on these coordinates now. They should be dropping right into our ranks. We can't afford to have it packed asses to elbows down here—we'd be slaughtered." He rose from his chair.

"I have no authority over you, my friends. But circumstance has united us in arms against a vicious and deadly foe. It's a war of extermination; without treaties, without quarter. Either we kill the S'Cotar or they kill us—every man, woman and child in the galaxy. We can't make any mistakes. There are no second chances.

"Please, follow my and my officers' orders explicitly. We

don't harbor delusions of cultural or intellectual superiority.
But when it comes to fighting this particular plague, we're
experts. We have the scars to prove it.

"Agreed?"

"We're with you," said Sutherland. "What choice do we
have?" he added, firmly shaking D'Trelna's hand. "What are
your instructions, Captain?"

"Select your men from the military force topside, Mr.
Sutherland," said the K'Ronarin. "Take them to the supply
shuttle—it's the third one on the beach—for weapons. Brief
them, then have them report here to me."

With a nod, Bill led his team from the room, wondering
what he'd tell the square-jawed infantry Colonel now uselessly
deploying his men along the hill. A lie couched in truth, probably. It usually worked.

"I'll command the ground action," D'Trelna said as the
door closed. "Commander K'Raoda will continue trying to
activate the defenses. If I'm killed, he'll assume command,
followed by Sergeant D'Nir of my commandos.

"Now, gather around, please." He spread a map of the
installation out on top of the equipment. "Let me explain our
strategy—such as it is."

Montanoya hung up the phone. "We can't contact Goose
Hill or Otis," he said to the other man in the Oval Office.
"Best we can do is raise one of the bridge blockades or that
destroyer off Falmouth. The Cape's undergoing some very
sophisticated jamming." The calmness of his voice surprised
him.

Sixtyish, Mexican-American, one of his country's finest career ambassadors before becoming National Security Advisor,
Montanoya felt powerless. It wasn't the aliens or the
K'Ronarins or the pending battle; it was the lack of data. The
future of his planet, the survival of humanity were being decided on a spit of land five hundred miles north and he didn't
know what was happening.

"Should we send more troops?" asked Doug MacDonald,
the first liberal Democrat president in four terms. At present,
MacDonald looked haggard, in spite of his Southern California

good looks. He hadn't slept or eaten since the whole madness started.

"Last word we had was that most of our forces were withdrawing at the K'Ronarins' request. Seems we're not equipped for a thirtieth-century war."

"I can't take this, José. The entire course of human history's being decided out there and here we sit, waiting for the damn phone to ring." He nodded curtly. "The hell with it. Have them call Andrews and ready Air Force One. We're going to Cape Cod."

Montanoya protested, despite feeling similar sentiments. "I wish you'd reconsider, sir. Evidently that place's going to be hell on earth soon. Given the type of weapons used—"

MacDonald cut him short. "The entire character of civilization is already being altered, José. Just contacting an alien culture will change it. And under these traumatic circumstances, none of us may survive the experience.

"No." He turned from the window. "I'm of no use here—I might as well be in the thick of it.

"You don't have to come, José," he added gently.

Montanoya's sallow complexion grew even darker. "You didn't say that when we were boarding an LST for Omaha Beach, Doug," he said softly. "I'll forget you said it now."

He walked over to FDR's mahogany desk and picked up the phone.

"Enemy contact, sir," reported the crewman to L'Wrona's right.

"Let's have a look," the XO ordered.

The battlescreen flared into life. Five darting needles rushed in V formation over the Earth's curve, rapidly closing on the much larger arrow of *Implacable*.

"Battlestations. Stand by Weapons crews." L'Wrona keyed into Tactics. Glancing at the readout, he said, "Message to ground force. 'Enemy contact. Five Deadeye class fighters. We are engaging. Message ends.'"

"Ninety seconds to weapons range," N'Trol reported from the Tactics console.

Three of the needles peeled off, dropping away. The other two continued straight toward *Implacable*.

"Message to ground force," said L'Wrona. "'Be advised three enemy interceptors on heading Terra. Message ends.'"

"Stand by to engage. Independent fire."

An instant later the serenity of space was torn by streaking missile and probing beam.

"Here they come!" cried D'Nir, looking up from the portable detector screen.

D'Trelna bounded from K'Raoda's side to the detector. A quick look was all he needed.

"Tactical," he snapped. "Everyone get below. We're about to be blasted by S'Cotar fighters."

"I'm getting too old for this," wheezed McShane as he and John ran from the hilltop down the rocky path to the tunnel's blasted entrance. The passageway was filled with tense men adjusting warsuits and checking weapons. There was little conversation.

From his position at the detector screen, D'Trelna watched as the sleek black fighters dived on Goose Hill, dropped small glowing orbs of destruction, then wheeled, clawing for altitude as the greatest explosion yet rocked the hill.

"That's to cut off our retreat!" shouted the Captain above the roar. John and Bob burst into the room.

"The proverbial kitchen sink?" asked Bob.

"Small version of a planetbuster," D'Trelna said. "Very small."

K'Raoda was still coolly entering series after series of Imperial computer codes into the terminal as fast as they flashed over the screen from *Implacable*'s archives.

D'Trelna alerted the men waiting in the passageway. "Any second now they'll start materializing. Good luck." Drawing his sidearm, he checked it, then laid it carefully on the console.

"And good luck to you, old friend," said John, leaving to join Zahava and Greg in the tunnel. He gave the older man a fond hug.

"Keep your head down," growled the professor. "You haven't got your degree yet.

"How close do they have to be to teleport, Captain?" he asked, turning to the officer as the door slid shut.

"Technically, from anywhere on the planet or in orbit. But I'll bet their staging area is nearby. They have to rally transmutes and warriors from across Terra, brief them and launch a coordinated attack. Nearby." He nodded.

"And, Professor, they'll be very damned good."

John and Zahava stood diagonally opposite each other in the passageway, a pattern repeated one hundred yards to either side of the transport room.

(K'Raoda, briefly leaving his post to help position the men, had cheerfully told Zahava the formation's name: Last Ditch Gambit. "Delays but never stops them.")

Each end of the formation was anchored by two small, floating spheres, constantly patrolling back and forth, up and down. Six more of the machines guarded the length and breadth of the vaulted ceiling above the men's heads. On their usefulness the Captain had had a few words earlier.

"Good only for the first wave or two, but they will take the edge from the enemy's advantage of surprise.

"After thirty seconds, the guard spheres will self-destruct—the S'Cotar can reprogram small robots. We'd be cut down by our own guns."

The S'Cotar were in the corridor, firing as they materialized.

John snapped a shot into the nearest warrior. The bolt burned through a mandible, boring into the alien's brain. Dying, its twitching tentacles sent a deadly blue beam glancing harmlessly off John's warsuit. As the insectoid fell, he turned, parrying a knife thrust with his rifle.

The pattern of one-on-one combat was being repeated the length of the passageway, as hellish energies again gouged into the scarred tunnel rock, blasting through flesh and stone with impunity.

The guard spheres, their time up, died, sinking to the floor with a soft *whoosh*. One landed next to where Greg and a warrior fought, the man trying to keep the insectoid's pincers from his throat, the alien straining to keep the other's knife from its gut.

The battle soon disintegrated as more and more S'Cotar arrived, the humans disappearing beneath struggling piles of S'Cotar.

The corridor nearly secured, a party of warriors directed by a transmute began working on the transport room door, burning into it with a large, semiportable blaster.

"Not long now," said D'Trelna, watching the battle on his monitor. Picking up his blaster, he turned to face the now-glowing door.

McShane lifted a rifle from beside K'Raoda and quietly joined *Implacable*'s Captain. "Civilization, my friend, usually requires old men to die quietly, antiseptically. I thank you for letting me go with good friends in an epic stand for humanity. It's something given to few." He clicked the safety off.

"Sir!" called K'Raoda, looking up. "I think—"

"Might as well draw your sidearm and join us, Subcommander," said D'Trelna. His eyes were riveted on the door, now glowing a fierce red. Waves of heat washed into the room. "Keep to one side. They've got a semi going."

"Captain," the Tactics Officer said sharply, not obeying, "I've received an acknowledgment from—"

The S'Cotar were gone.

Like that.

After a stunned moment, those of the defenders who could rise did so, looking uncertainly about.

"Where'd they go?" called Sutherland, helping Bakunin out from under a dead warrior. The KGB officer retrieved his blade from the S'Cotar's thorax, wiping it on the corpse and returning it to his boot sheath.

"Far, far away, I hope," he said wearily.

"You can thank Subcommander K'Raoda for our deliverance," said D'Trelna, exiting through the still-smoldering but operable transport room doorway. "He seems to have aroused the computer."

"Indeed he has, Captain," said a deep, resonant voice. It was the same rich contralto Zahava, Bob, Greg and John had last heard ordering them into the transport web. "I've sent the S'Cotar where they'll do no further harm."

"Identify yourself," snapped D'Trelna, looking about. He

could spot no speakers anywhere, yet the voice filled the corridor.

"I am Planetary Operations Control System, Mode Six, programmed by the Imperial Colonial Service on K'Ronar, Imperium 2028," the unruffled voice responded.

K'Raoda's jaw dropped. "Captain, that was . . ."

"I know. Five thousand years ago, more or less."

"Where did you send the S'Cotar, computer?"

"My operational acronym is POCSYM Six, Captain. As for the enemy, they've been placed in the center of the sun."

"Why did you take so long to respond?" demanded K'Raoda.

"Can you defend this planet against further attack?" the Captain asked.

"Please, gentlemen," demurred POCSYM. "First let me assure you that there is no further danger of direct assault.

"Secondly, with your permission, let me convey the dead and wounded to *Implacable* and yourselves to comfortable quarters, where we can talk."

D'Trelna cast a glance at where two medics, Terran and K'Ronarin, were doing what they could for the wounded— fully a fifth of the human force. He tried to ignore the still, shrouded forms lying along the wall, but couldn't.

"All right." The Captain sighed. "But I must speak with my ship."

"You're already in touch with them, Captain," said POCSYM. "Every word of this conversation and a video are being transmitted to your bridge."

"D'Trelna to *Implacable*. What is your status?"

L'Wrona's voice filled not just the commnet but the air as well. "All secure, sir. All enemy craft disappeared—they didn't go into hyperspace. They just vanished. Could POCSYM have—"

"You assume correctly, Commander L'Wrona. I transported all attack craft to the same place as their ground force."

"Pouff!" exclaimed Bakunin, with a gesture.

"'Pouff' to many familiar things soon, Colonel," said Sutherland, tiredly removing his helmet. "Including, I suspect, the dictatorship of the proletariat."

"Very well," D'Trelna said. "Transport when ready."

The Goose Hill site stood empty.

"'Any sufficiently advanced technology is indistinguishable from magic,'" quoted McShane, opening his eyes.

His first impression was of a big room awash with sunlight, the air redolent of roses. Baroque music was playing.

Looking around, he filled in the gaps: the room was large, comfortably furnished in flawlessly sculpted teak, a long, luxuriant table its centerpiece; there were roses, four bouquets of American beauties gracing the side tables beneath bay windows; and it was music of the Baroque period, possibly Vivaldi. No devotee of the period, McShane reserved judgment.

"Vivaldi, I think," said John. "One of the *Seasons*."

The others, equally tattered, tired and begrimed, stood silently drinking in the room's subdued elegance. John glanced out a window and started.

"Who are those men?" he asked. "And what are they building?"

They all turned to look. In a hollow, perhaps a mile away, thousands of tiny figures labored atop three huge stone terraces, busily constructing a fourth.

"Nabopolassar throws a tower to heaven in honor of Marduk," said POCSYM. "When it's done, it will have eight stories totaling two hundred and eighty-eight feet and contain a statue of Marduk cast in twenty-six tons of pure gold. It will be thrown down by Xerxes, pondered over by Alexander and partially restored by Koldewy."

"The Tower of Babel," breathed McShane.

"Yes, Professor," POCSYM confirmed. "*Etemenanki*— the Tower of Babel. Classical hubris at its height. I thought it might entertain you.

"I have videos of all major human works and disasters of the past fifty centuries. The destruction of Sodom and Gomorrah is particularly affecting, but not before dinner, which now awaits."

Turning back to the room, they saw the table now groaning under a vast selection of steaming entrées, some Terran, some K'Ronarin.

"I've attempted to select food from each culture which would be palatable to the other," said POCSYM.

"POCSYM," John said wearily, "we've no wish to be impolite, but we are a bit travel-stained." Their warsuits were caked with green slime and dirt. "Might we wash up?"

"Of course, Mr. Harrison. I've been remiss as a host.

"Through the door"—an exit appeared where a wall had been—"are the old staff quarters. Each room has toilet facilities. Two men to a room."

As they filed out, POCSYM added, "No need to hurry—I'll put the food in stasis." The steam stopped in midrise over the food.

"Actually, this works out rather well," said the computer, its voice accompanying them down the broad, mosaic-tiled corridor. "The wines will have a chance to breathe."

"This can't be five thousand years old!" protested Greg, waving his long-stemmed crystal wineglass. "It looks new."

Something light, airy and Viennese played merrily in the background: *Roses from the South*.

"All but my basic monitoring and defense clusters were in stasis until just before dinner, Mr. Farnesworth," said POCSYM. "Although on a very passive, almost subconscious level, I was observing your group's activities."

"You avoided a question before dinner, POCSYM," said the Captain, eating what Zahava was sure must be either sautéed eel or snake. Like the rest, he now wore coveralls bearing the insignia of the Imperial Colonial Service: clasped hands surmounting a silver-wreathed planet.

"Why did you wait so long to intervene? You saw our casualties."

"I regret the delay, Captain," the earnest baritone responded. "But it took some while to determine that you were actually the legitimate heirs to the Imperium and then to activate my defense circuits. Recall that I've been on standby for fifty centuries."

"Can you defend Terra?" asked Sutherland.

"Can and have, sir, within certain limitations, but only if so ordered by the senior K'Ronarin officer."

"So ordered," said D'Trelna between mouthfuls.

"Where are we now?" John asked, pushing away the

chicken Kiev and pouring himself another glass of Château
Lafite-Rothschild 1947.

"Colonial Service's first Operations center on the planet.
One of the better port facilities on Terra and a natural trading
center. You are two miles below the Isle of Manhattan."

Despite the wonder of it all, excited talk soon gave way to
nodding heads and slurred syllables: food, drink and exhaustion combined to send the humans, singly and in groups, filter-
ing from the dining area to their rooms.

Leaving hand in hand, John and Zahava were almost to their
door when POCSYM asked, "Care for a history lesson?"

"Not tonight," said Zahava as the door slid open. "We're
tired."

"I can instruct as you sleep. Subliminal teaching is both
effective and painless."

"Fine," said John, following Zahava into the room. "See
you in the morning—or whatever." The door closed.

"Pardon my Jewish paranoia," Zahava whispered a few
minutes later, slipping her dark nakedness into John's bunk,
"but is POCSYM our only ticket out of here?"

"Sure sounds like it," he said, sliding a hand down her slim
back till it rested atop a soft, round cheek. He gave a fond
squeeze. "I didn't see an exit sign. We'd best be nice to him
. . . it."

"You're supposed to be exhausted," Zahava said as John's
other hand came into play.

"Most of me is," he confided, pulling her on top of him.

"Satyr," she whispered huskily as his hands caressed her.

The lights dimmed discreetly out.

CHAPTER 13

HUGE, SILENT, THE SHIPS landed at night, far from the great river valleys with their rude villages. Disgorging armies of men and machines, they left—all but three.

It was a task of years before flaring energy beams and deep set atomics finished the enormous caverns that would house the Project. By then the Staff had begun.

Men would disappear from their hovels, reappearing months later to speak slowly and strongly of new ideas, new gods, of better ways to live. At first some of them were killed, denounced as heretics, witches, devils. But most lived on to change the lives of their peoples. And once it was known that those who opposed the new men died—always of natural causes—effective resistance ceased.

The seed had been sown.

Through the centuries it was carefully nurtured and cultivated, becoming the root from which civilization sprang. The arts and sciences came into being and flourished. Temples and monuments were raised. Priesthoods and dynasties were founded, growing into greatness. The time for cross-fertilization had come.

Trade, before confined to land and coastal routes, now spread across the great waters, aided by new discoveries and navigation: devices that always showed a true heading, and simple instruments to determine position by sun and stars.

Often, touching upon some strange new shore, the mariners found their gods already there, housed in familiar small temples. And nearby hunters, farmers and fishermen, friendly and eager to trade.

Among the natives there lived, invariably, one man who spoke the mariners' language and knew their customs: the village shaman, versed in the ways of the gods the two peoples found they shared.

Goods and ideas flowed smoothly, the seafarers sharing the techniques of the Bronze Age with the landsmen. Their culture came, over the centuries, to resemble more and more that of the mariners.

Bonds of kinship developed through intermarriage. What often began as an arrangement between two peoples would become a trading confederation, expanding until it met other confederations with similar origins. In time, these allied confederations bound a continent. All prospered.

East across the ocean went gold, copper, silver, furs and hides. West came bronze tools, weapons, luxury goods.

An objective analysis of this cultural melding would have shown that at each critical stage, either a shaman in the West or a high priest in the East—or both—served as a catalyst. But the only social scientists around were themselves orchestrating the process.

The time came, at last, to begin the next Phase: technological refinements designed to tighten the bonds between East and West, eventually urbanizing the westerners. Steam engines and storage batteries were "invented" simultaneously in several eastern kingdoms. Before they could be refined, however, the Recall came.

It was the Senior Developmental Anthropologist's final year of his twenty-year tour on the planet. He took pride in the fact that of all preceding S.D.A.'s, his was one of only three stewardships under which a Phase had begun. The preparation had taken a long, hard decade. He was looking forward to his return to D'Lin, headquarters of the Colonial Service, and a well-earned retirement to a small, verdant archipelago on a water world of Sector Yellow.

The anthropologist, whose name was R'Garna, looked up, startled at the four beeps preceding an emergency subspace message. A holograph of the Colonial Minister, his face lined and haggard, filled the wall.

"This is a general address message." Despite a distance of

hundreds of light-years, the equipment faithfully recreated his exhausted tone. "All stations, all sections, all commands will cease operations at once and fall back to D'Lin.

"Rebel forces have overrun all but Sectors Green and Yellow. Use extreme caution—the loyalty of all forces but the Home Fleet is in doubt. God save the Emperor. Good luck." His image dissolved.

R'Garna sighed deeply, sadly shaking his balding head. Old age had finally caught up with the K'Ronarin Empire. Sector governors had been seceding—successfully—for the past fifty years. The Recall could only mean that last month's rumor of a savage mauling of the Home Fleet by Z'Kalan rebels under ex-Governor S'Tren was true.

As a social scientist, the S.D.A. saw no end to the accelerating collapse of Pax Galactica. Anarchy would reign, and then would begin a long, painful climb back to the stars. He'd been careful to keep this opinion from the omnipresent ears of Security.

R'Garna knew also, as a veteran of two multifleet "police actions," that should he live to reach D'Lin, his reserve commission would be quickly activated. He had grave doubts about ever seeing his lush archipelago.

POCSYM hurled the two ships from their rocky wombs, deep into space. From there they began the first of a series of homeward-bound jumps, some through the middle of rebel sectors. Months later, badly shot up, one of them would limp into besieged D'Lin, half her complement dead. R'Garna's ship didn't make it.

Its masters gone, POCSYM placed all but its own considerable equipment in stasis, against the day of their return. It then turned to monitoring the Recall's effect on the plans and work of centuries. It didn't like what it saw, but was forbidden to intervene.

Lack of speedier transportation prevented a massive infusion of new blood from the West into the atrophying social structures of the East. Losing their vitality, the old dynasties fell to the brash young neighbors they'd before controlled with ease. Trade ceased and the tall ships went out no more.

In the West, the prosperity brought by the mariners departed with them. The confederations disintegrated. Tribes bickered and fought, some slipping back to a seminomadic existence, others descending into the barbarism of human sacrifice. All fell easy prey, much later, to eastern men who no longer came in peace.

POCSYM detected the S'Cotar fleet when it first came out of hyperspace. It activated its defenses and waited—*this* was a problem it could confront.

When the aliens were within easy range, POCSYM casually transported all ships to the same half mile of space.

It did so with the next two fleets that appeared over the next decade. There was an interlude of peace.

The K'Ronarins weren't the only ones, though, capable of finding and refitting old Imperial ships. Using such a vessel, the S'Cotar gave the appropriate recognition codes and landed far from civilization. Destroying their ship, the transmutes scattered across the globe. Congratulating themselves on penetrating POCSYM's defenses, they began their search for the computer.

Over the next half century, they found and destroyed many of the small transporter/temple sites, used by the Colonial Service teams for intraplanetary movement and training of locals. They had no luck, though, in finding any of the main bases.

POCSYM was able to subtly alter their detector readings. Twice, the S'Cotar thought they'd scanned an underground installation. Each time, their assault force teleported into solid rock, miles below the surface. No third attempt was made.

Knowing they couldn't seize Terra until POCSYM was taken out, and finding their resources to do so inadequate, the S'Cotar established a base on a Martian satellite. From there, they augmented their force on Earth, teleporting at great risk through POCSYM's defenses. Thus reinforced, the insectoids infiltrated key posts in one of the more powerful Terran states. With its resources clandestinely at their disposal, the S'Cotar hoped to locate and quietly destroy the pesky computer. *Implacable*'s unexpected arrival and the imminent discovery of a functioning transporter site by the Terrans had forced the S'Cotar into a premature battle. . . .

CHAPTER 14

JOHN AWOKE TO something soft beating him in the face. Reaching out, he wrested the small, round pillow from Zahava's hands.

"Mouth breather!" she accused. "You were snoring!" She slid from his grasp, stepping onto the deep-carpeted floor. "Pleasant dreams?" she asked, ducking into the bathroom.

"Enlightening, perhaps. Shouldn't believe everything you dream, though." Rising, he looked for his clothes. "Seems to be a pilferage problem," he grumbled, not finding them.

"You'll find fresh Colonial Service uniforms in the wardrobe," advised POCSYM's voice.

"Do you always eavesdrop?" He opened the wardrobe door. Duplicates of last night's attire, clean and flawlessly pressed, hung there. Warsuits and blasters lay neatly stacked atop a shelf.

"Actually, yes. It's my programming. I'm sorry if it offends you."

"What time is it?" asked John.

"Ten-ten A.M., eastern standard time."

"Do you keep track of the time in each zone?" he asked, poking about the wardrobe's shelves.

"No. I listen to a lot of FM—mostly classical," confessed POCSYM. "I got the time check from one of the Manhattan stations."

"Oh."

"Yes, I've monitored radio and television transmissions since their inception. It helps keep me abreast of the geopoliti-

93

cal situation, and allows me to record changes in the mores and folkways of the various cultures.

"I have statistical evidence, in fact, that minor changes in social mores are frequently engineered by the media."

"Comforting," drawled John, ending his search of the wardrobe. "You wouldn't happen to have a razor, would you?"

"Depilatory cream is on the third shelf behind the bath mirror. You should find all necessary toiletries there."

Before John could move, Zahava closed the bathroom door. A shower started.

"Anyone else up yet?" he asked.

"I am," boomed a voice. Bob came in, looking a bit absurd in his Colonial Service uniform. "Don't let our pompous wizard bamboozle you," he said, jerking a thumb toward the wall. "For all its supposed scientific objectivity, it's accumulated an extraordinary number of operatic recordings. It favored me with an original cut of Caruso in *The Barber of Seville*—Caruso, John! God only knows how he . . . it . . . got it."

Sitting on his bunk, tugging on a boot, John grunted, "We all have pronoun problems with Mr. POCSYM.

"Were you given the same dream as we were?" he asked, squeezing his left foot into the tight-fitting K'Ronarin boot.

"Mighty ships, pigmy humans, Imperial *noblesse oblige*?" Bob smiled.

"You doubt?" asked John, rising.

"Someone should be a doubting Thomas. I'm bunked with D'Trelna and that cynical old space dog ate it up. If he did, the rest probably did.

"Oh, I accept all this"—he waved a vague hand about—"*a priori*. Direct evidence and the reasoned judgment of our intellect says this isn't a Borges fantasy. But we have only POCSYM's word for this revisionist history—three-dimensional and in living color though it may be. No, I reserve judgment. You?"

"The same. Logic compels caution. We've been thrust into the midst of a galactic war whose—"

The bathroom door vanished. Steam billowed in, a naked form dimly visible through the mist. Bob's hasty exit ended the conversation.

At breakfast, John asked a question that'd been nagging him. "CIA and KGB, working as a team?" His gaze shifted between Bakunin and Sutherland. "Things must really have changed since I left. You'll put yourselves out of a job."

Zahava and Greg looked up with interest. McShane, listening intently to K'Raoda, took no notice.

"Not really our fault," said Sutherland between mouthfuls of what looked like fresh blueberry blintzes, bacon and coffee. "It started with Admiral Canaris's Abwehr," he said, naming the Third Reich's military intelligence arm.

"Abwehr stumbled onto a site very much like the one at Goose Hill." Bakunin picked up the tale. "It was used by the French Resistance as a storage and staging area. An Abwehr raiding party arrived at the site just as what we now know were S'Cotar transmutes dropped in —probably looking for POC SYM." He paused, sipping coffee.

Sutherland pushed his plate away with a contented sigh. "The meeting between the Nazis and the S'Cotar was Hobbesian: 'nasty, brutish and short.' The bugs teleported away, destroying the site as they left. Only one of the Abwehr unit lived through the carnage. He carried a map, snatched from the S'Cotar, showing the probable locations of POCSYM's transporter sites."

"An SS officer got the map," said Bakunin, picking up the story, "then gave it to us and the Americans after the war. By that time, though, all the sites we could find had been destroyed. As proved true with the CIA's explorations."

"Why did you and the Russians cooperate, Bill?" asked Greg. "Especially during the cold war." Unnoticed, the window now showed a red-sailed galley skimming an azure sea. High above its fifty-oared deck, something gold caught the sun.

"Each side was sobered," said Sutherland, stirring cognac into his coffee, "by the way those transporter sites had been destroyed. Someone—something—used energy weapons far beyond our ken." He watched the cream curdle to the surface.

"Confronted by this, we didn't rush to embrace like kids trapped in a wild storm—not *quite*. Let's just say that on this topic, and this topic alone, there's been a warm rapprochement over the years, carried on at the highest levels of government."

"I have a question for the good Captain," said John, appropriating some of Sutherland's cognac. "If the S'Cotar can teleport—and we know they can—why did they storm Goose Hill a second time? Why not just teleport in and blow us to pieces while we were still outside? They had the location from their first attack."

D'Trelna, seated next to McShane, was puffing on one of Bob's cigars. He removed the panatela from his mouth, thoughtfully regarding its profile before answering.

"Frankly, I don't know. And I don't like it. Their entire method of operation has been different in your solar system. Downright incompetent, really. All we can do is hope that they continue that way, for whatever reason." He stuck the cigar back into his mouth.

"Another question," said Zahava. "How do you explain the invisibility of all those warriors over the years? If, as you say, they're nontelepaths, how could they maintain a protective illusion?"

"I think I can answer that," said K'Raoda, pushing his empty plate away. "They didn't.

"They were probably all housed in one central place—I suspect the Institute—until needed. Two or three of the transmutes could project an image of normalcy throughout the entire installation whenever there were visitors."

"It looks like the surface of the moon," said MacDonald to Montanoya as the two men looked down on Goose Hill. The morning sun had woven a grotesque tapestry of light and shadow from the twisted alien bodies and molten, wide-strewn rubble.

"More like something out of Dante, Mr. President," said Montanoya.

"Land where you can," MacDonald ordered the air force Major piloting the Apache gunship.

"Where you can" was next to a pair of gutted K'Ronarin scout craft. The six escort gunships settled in a protective ring around the presidential chopper.

Following a combat-ready platoon of Secret Servicemen, they made their way up from the beach to where S'Cotar bodies heaped the blasted entrance.

"Don't look much prettier burned than they do intact," said Montanoya, comparing a charred corpse to one less damaged.

"There are probably many life forms in the universe, José," said MacDonald, waiting for their escort to check the site. "Perhaps we're as repulsive to them as they are to us."

"No one home, Mr. President," reported the agent in charge five minutes later. "Something sure blasted the hell out of the lower corridor and the room above it, though. No human bodies, but plenty of *them*." He nudged a headless corpse with the polished black toe of his combat boot.

"Okay. Let's have a look," MacDonald said.

Armed men front and rear, the President and Montanoya carefully picked their way down the rubble-strewn stairs and upper corridor, through the broken remains of the altar chamber, then down the ladder to the lower tunnel, its lighting flickering on and off. The scarred walls and blasted S'Cotar corpses bore mute testimony to the hellish energies that had raged there.

MacDonald turned to the escort commander. "Where was—"

He never finished the question. He and Montanoya disappeared, leaving consternation in their wake.

"And this is Central Control," said POCSYM to the humans entering the large room.

Screens above unmanned consoles came on, filling with sights both familiar and strange. London, New York, Moscow, Paris, Tokyo, Singapore, Rio de Janeiro, Bonn, the North American continent, Terra, Terra and its moon, the outer planets, the sun.

"Are those real or taped?" asked the Russian, peering closely at Mars. The color and clarity were flawless.

"Real, Colonel. I've maintained the satellite observation network first installed by Fleet. Drone repair ships are on station in the asteroids and many of the planetary satellites."

The screens blanked out.

"We're about to receive visitors, gentlemen and lady. Please stand well away from the center of the room," POCSYM requested. "And no matter what you think you see, do nothing."

Sutherland was still in awe of the seemingly effortless way POCSYM transmitted and reassembled people. With no apparent transition, José Montanoya and President MacDonald stood in the center of the room, blinking.

"Welcome to K'Ronarin Planetary Command," said POCSYM. "I've been looking forward to this meeting for some time."

"You have the advantage, sir," MacDonald said, taking in the unfamiliar faces.

"Your pardon, sir. I am POCSYM Six, this installation's guardian."

"I'm José Montanoya," said the National Security Advisor. He paused. Why didn't Sutherland do or say something? The man was just standing there, staring at him. "And this gentleman"—he indicated MacDonald—"is the President of the United States, where I hope we still are."

"You are in the United States, or rather under it, Mr. Montanoya," replied POCSYM. "But your companion is neither gentle nor a man. Stand away from him, please."

Ignoring the hisses of indrawn breath and weapons being drawn, POCSYM continued, "Greetings to you, Gaun-Sharick, Illusion Master of the Infinite Hosts of the Magnificent. Hail! and well met, ancient foe."

"No!" cried Montanoya, even as he backed away from MacDonald. "I've known this man for forty years. He can't be an . . . alien."

"See and believe, Mr. Montanoya," POCSYM said.

MacDonald's form shimmered for an instant, then was replaced by a transmute. The alien stood unmoving. It carried no weapons.

"And the President?" asked Montanoya after a moment's stunned silence. "What about the President?"

Dead, said a voice in all their heads. The S'Cotar turned its huge eyes on them. *We held him in our base on Demos. Your newfound friends killed him in their rush to destroy us.*

"Intellectually, Gaun-Sharick is as old as I am, if you discount the hundreds of successive clones through which his persona has passed," POCSYM said. "He stands high in the Council of the Magnificent. His is the task of exterminating all hostile—that is to say alien—life. If he can sow dissension among the foes of the Host, all the better. He's the father of lies.

"Didn't you wonder, Mr. Montanoya," asked POCSYM, "why on earth, or under it, a President of the United States would expose himself to danger, especially without media coverage?

"Gaun-Sharick hoped I would be fooled into transporting him here. Talks between the Terrans and the K'Ronarins was, of course, the next logical step.

"Behold the Illusion Master, stripped of his illusions.

"Captain D'Trelna," POCSYM addressed the Confederation officer, who stood with blaster leveled at the insectoid, "please tell the Terrans what must have occurred for Gaun-Sharick to have imitated their President so well."

Clearing his throat, the Captain complied. "His memories had to be transferred, down to the most basic level, directly into the alien's mind. This is accomplished by slowly inserting the thin, hard antennae concealed in the mandibles into the victim's brain, absorbing each successive layer of memory even as the victim dies. The process takes several very painful hours."

The horrified silence was broken by Montanoya trying to seize John's blaster.

"No, Mr. Montanoya!" said POCSYM. "Alive he can be used to avenge your friend. Dead he is of no use. Something he realizes—he's tried to teleport continuously in the last minute. It would be certain death, as he doesn't know his location. I've blocked those attempts as well as his efforts to bring unwelcome visitors. With your permission, Captain, I'll put him on a debriefer."

"What's that?" asked Greg.

"It will extract every bit of data from his mind, but unlike your President, the process won't kill Gaun-Sharick," said K'Raoda. "I assume there's an Imperial model here. Much more thorough than ours—it will leave him a vegetable." There was no mercy in the young officer's voice.

D'Trelna gestured to two of his commandos. They came up to the alien, flanking him. "Follow the blue light to Interrogation, gentlemen,'' directed POCSYM. ''My robots will take charge of the prisoner there.''

A ball of soft blue light, a foot in diameter, appeared on the floor before prisoner and escort, slowly moving toward the door. The trio followed.

Gaun-Sharick turned at the door, transfixing them with baleful red eyes, twin pools of malevolence. His voice hissed in their minds again. *We shall write your names on water. The scattering dust is your fate.* The door closed behind him.

''Now what?'' asked a shaken José Montanoya.

''I suggest we await our battle fleet, sir, then negotiate a mutual defense treaty,'' D'Trelna said. ''It's only a matter of time before the S'Cotar bring up their main force. Our presence here confirms the importance of Terra and this system.'' He nodded at a wall hologram of the solar system.

''What is that blue light orbiting Earth?'' asked Bob. ''*Implacable*?''

''Yes,'' POCSYM said. ''Blue is friendly, red hostile. Shall we continue the tour?''

CHAPTER 15

Implacable's XO reread the commscan:

MOST URGENT
From: Grand Admiral L'Guan
        Vigilant
To: Captain D'Trelna
        Implacable
II Sector Fleet and elements Home Fleet enroute
your position. Be advised massive repeat massive
enemy withdrawals from occupied sectors. Enemy
converging on your position. You are to defend the
planet Terra until relieved. If, in your judgment,
position becomes untenable, you will retreat only
after destroying all Imperial equipment on Terra.
END

"Maximum detector watch. Maintain high alert," L'Wrona
ordered the incoming watch as he eyed the screen. *Implacable*
still showed as the only ship in the system. "Better get me the
Captain."

Dwarfed by the huge ship, the men stood craning their
necks, trying to gauge her size.

"A mile high, at least," marveled John, taking in the vast
expanse of gray metal, bulging with weapons blisters and instrument pods.

"A mile and a quarter, actually," corrected POCSYM.

"And eight miles long. Designed for space but transported here by me, under orders."

"Magnificent," D'Trelna breathed. "I don't recognize her class, but she's certainly one of the great Imperial dreadnoughts. Why didn't they take her with them, POCSYM?"

There was a moment's silence, as if the computer were debating itself. If so, it reached a decision.

"They couldn't, Captain. She was exiled here, to the Empire's outer marches, greatest and last of the symbiotechnic battleships."

D'Trelna stepped back with a gasp. K'Raoda's eyes widened and his jaw dropped. A murmur of disgust swept the K'Ronarins.

"A mindslaver!" D'Trelna finally managed.

"If you will, Captain," said POCSYM with distaste. "But not just any . . . 'mindslaver.' She is *Revenge*. Does that name still mean something to you?"

The Terrans, lost by this exchange, saw that the name did indeed mean something to their allies. It flew from lip to lip.

"Only one ship has ever borne that name," said the Captain slowly. "*T'Nil's Revenge.*"

"What's all this about?" asked Bob.

> "T'Nil's Revenge, great ship of woe
> To distant time, to greater cause
> Must she need go"

quoted K'Raoda. "I always thought it just some childish doggerel," he added.

"You see before you a legend, Professor," said D'Trelna, hand sweeping the vessel. "*T'Nil's Revenge*, politely known as a symbiotechnic dreadnought, commonly called a mindslaver. Bigger, faster, deadlier than any battleship since her ancient day. And totally outlawed. To build a mindslaver or to research mindslaver technology carries the death penalty—a punishment otherwise reserved for high treason."

"What, pray tell, is a 'mindslaver'?" demanded an exasperated Sutherland.

"A ship having, as its various cognitive cores, disembodied

human minds,'' POCSYM said. "Such vessels enjoyed vast superiority in Weapons, Maneuver and Tactics. Properly maintained, the mindslaves were virtually immortal.''

"You might tell them the rest, POCSYM,'' said K'Raoda. "How such minds went quietly mad, unable to die, living only for combat, the thrill of killing. How they were controlled by technicians mindlinked with them. Of the toll it took on those men.''

"This is the last mindslaver?'' asked John.

"Yes,'' POCSYM said. "The rest were destroyed as a mercy by the selfsame T'Nil whose revenge she embodies.''

"How so?'' asked Zahava.

"The *Annals* say only that criminals were killing people and selling their brains for use in warships,'' said K'Raoda. "T'Nil, then Admiral T'Nil, brought them to justice and was crowned Emperor by a grateful people.''

POCSYM laughed.

The humans looked up, startled, as the resonant laughter boomed through the cavern.

"I'm sorry,'' POCSYM apologized, recovering. "You just reminded me, Subcommander, of what a Terran general once said when asked what history would say of him. 'History, sir, will tell lies,' he said.

"Let me tell you the truth, gentlehumans, about *Revenge* and T'Nil and the Mindslavers Guild. My truth.

"Once upon a time, many thousands of years ago, there were space pirates, raiding K'Ronarin shipping and small colonies. Each year the problem grew worse, with Fleet never able to catch more than an occasional small pirate ship. The captured outlaws would usually confess to knocking over a few star-yachts, but even under mindprobe proved ignorant of the large, fleet-sized raids.

"The victims of these raids disappeared forever. Ransom was never asked.

"The attacks grew larger and bolder. Fleet, responding to the public outcry, built more and more of the new symbiotechnic dreadnoughts, equipped with the brains of convicts and the terminally ill. Within five years, fleets of these great ships were scouring the galaxy, searching for the brigands' base—a hopeless task, it seemed, given the vast number of possible hiding places, the dearth of accurate intelligence.

"Heeding the cries of anguished relatives and friends of the hundreds of thousands of missing colonists and spacemen, an already overtaxed Empire dug ever-deeper to build more ships to end the scourge.

"End it did—unexpectedly.

"A task force under Admiral L'Rar T'Nil—a cagey old war dog brought out of retirement to hunt down the pirates—a task force on routine patrol received a frantic distress call from the mining colony of R'Noa. Traveling at flank speed, T'Nil's force dropped out of hyperspace almost on top of the unsuspecting outlaw fleet—sleek vessels, bearing no insignia, but deployed in standard Fleet orbit pattern.

"Although taken by surprise, the brigands made a fierce stand.

"Only when T'Nil's marines finally stormed the bridge of the sole surviving hostile vessel did resistance end. And only then did the diabolical truth come to light.

"These were no 'pirates.' They were mindslavers—avaricious men ruthlessly collecting functioning human brains. Brains which they sold to Imperial Fleet contractors to build more mindslavers to hunt down the nonexistent pirates.

"The captured ship was a brainstrip facility. The colonists' brains were carefully removed and their empty, frozen bodies sold for surgical spare parts on the black market.

"The mindslavers had only partially scrubbed their records before dying. A complete list of their shareholders was recovered. It contained some of the most powerful and wealthy names in the Empire: senators, industrialists, financiers, senior officers, privy councilors, members of the royal family. All had profited handsomely from the venture.

"T'Nil was a brilliant strategist, and not just in space. He was adept at the political infighting that pervaded both Court and Fleet—'that fox,' the Emperor had once called him, unkindly.

"More, he commanded the close loyalty of his officers and men, for he'd been given back his old battlegroup, Task Force Forty-Seven. They'd followed the Admiral into hell more than once. Now he asked them to do so again, for he knew his command and life would be forfeit if he sent an honest report of the action.

"Task Force Forty-Seven disappeared into space, captured ship in tow.

"With unseemly haste, T'Nil and his men were proclaimed deserters and traitors, tried *in absentia* and sentenced to death.

"Two months later, raiders in Fleet uniform seized the civil communications station orbiting K'Ronar and broadcast graphic proof of all that I've just related to a horrified, sickened Empire: brainless, recognizable heads, holograms of the brainstrip vessel, airtight documentation.

"The ensuing popular revolt was brief but bloody enough for a general catharsis.

"Did I mention T'Nil's daughter? She was on R'Noa. Her father arrived too late to save her or his grandchildren.

"Even before his coronation, T'Nil rounded up all the masters of the *de facto* Mindslavers Guild. He had them brainstripped and placed aboard this vessel now before us. The other mindslaves were mercifully destroyed and the ships converted to conventional craft.

"Thus ends my truth, Subcommander," said POCSYM. "May it inform your own."

"Why was she sent here?" K'Raoda asked.

"I wasn't told. I suspect, though, that the disintegrating Empire didn't want *Revenge* falling into the hands of, say, a rebellious sector governor."

"And the mindslaves?" asked Bob.

"Functional, as is the rest of the ship. I've had her in stasis, of course. The mindslaves—"

The computer was checked by D'Trelna's upraised hand. "Yes?" the Captain said into his communicator.

"Sir, message from Admiral L'Guan." L'Wrona read it to him.

"I have something to add," said POCSYM. "Please check your detectors now, Commander. Do you confirm what my satellites have picked up?"

As L'Wrona turned toward the screen an ensign called, "Enemy force emerging from hyperspace."

Next to Pluto a swarm of tiny red dots were forming into a huge phalanx.

"S'Cotar battlefleet has entered from hyperspace near the ninth planet, sir," reported the XO. "They're dropping into assault wedge."

"How many?"

L'Wrona hopefully tapped the telltale. The figures didn't change. "Two thousand five hundred and twenty-eight," he reported stoically. "Heavy cruisers, destroyers, corsairs, scout and patrol craft, supply and transport vessels. Lots of transports. They're not just here for a casual visit."

"Where is the command ship?" asked the Captain.

"Can't tell at this range, sir."

"I have her, Captain," said POCSYM.

They were back in Central Control, facing a hologram of the solar system. "My apologies," the computer said, "but it seemed less cumbersome."

In the midst of the red dots now advancing on Earth glowed a single green light. "The command ship," said POCSYM. "She is *Nasqa*—'deadly wraith.' One mile in diameter, crew of three thousand."

"Well, Captain?" asked John.

D'Trelna was silent, eyes distant. He ran his fingers through thinning hair.

"POCSYM," he said finally, "can you defend Terra against such a massive force?"

"Gallantly, Captain, but very, very briefly."

"Can you put *Revenge* in orbit?"

"Yes, with ease."

"Can you put an assault team aboard *Nasqa* before her ships come within range of Terra?"

"Yes."

"My friends"—D'Trelna smiled—"let's adjourn to the meeting room and discuss a mad scheme I have. It's just insane enough to work."

"The hell you are!" John stormed at McShane. "You heard what the Captain said. His own men are afraid to mindlink with those creatures. What makes you so damned omnipotent?"

No sooner had D'Trelna announced his twofold "mad scheme" than Bob had volunteered for what John thought the most dangerous mission: mindlinking with the disembodied brains aboard *Revenge*.

The professor calmly regarded his angry ex-student. "I saw no rush of volunteers," he observed dryly.

"Also, I submit myself as the logical candidate." He poured water from an onyx carafe into a matching cup and sipped.

"It's been speculated that only Terrans, with their heart rate higher than K'Ronarin, have a chance of arriving aboard *Nasqa* undetected."

Speculated was the word for it. Two months ago the K'Ronarins had captured a S'Cotar courier ship. Along with new Fleet deployment and withdrawal protocols it carried modifications specs for ships' security systems. Henceforth, penetration alarms would be keyed only to the K'Ronarin heart rate. The S'Cotar had evidently been plagued by false intruder alerts triggered by too broad a detection program.

Rigging the courier's drive to overload, the K'Ronarins had blown the ship up along with her dead crew, hard by the S'Cotar advance. They could only hope the aliens had bought the accident, leaving the program modifications unchanged.

"Thus, all Terrans now here fit for combat may attempt entry. The surviving U.S. troopers left with Mr. Montanoya; his 'witnesses,' he called them."

"Despite the space spectacular, he'll need them if he wants to stay out of the funny farm," said Greg.

Bob smiled slightly. "Knowing the cobwebbed minds that clutter many senior government posts, I'm sure he will. If he appeared alone crying, 'Watch the sky! Watch the sky!' they'd put him in a rubber room.

"But that leaves only the five of you.

"As we know, the K'Ronarins refuse to meddle with what is to them abomination. The good Captain here will only ask his crew to man the less exotic parts of *Revenge*."

"Never give an order you know won't be obeyed," mumbled D'Trelna, sitting on the table's edge, eyes occasionally flicking to the screen and the advancing S'Cotar fleet.

"Further," continued Bob, "without the mindslaves and the

weapons systems they control, *Revenge* is just another ship. Correct, Captain?''

D'Trelna nodded.

''Someone who is expendable, unburdened by ancient legend and possessed of a disciplined mind must serve as mind-slave liaison. I am that man, gentlemen and lady. Hobson's choice: Take me or do without.''

Before anyone else could try to dissuade him, POCSYM spoke.

''*Nasqa* will be within transporter range in thirty minutes and her fleet within bombardment range of Terra in four hours. May I urge speed?''

''*Nasqa* assault group will don warsuits and arm. Be back here in twenty minutes for transport,'' ordered D'Trelna, rising.

''Crazy old coot,'' John muttered as he walked past McShane, affectionately squeezing the professor's shoulder.

Bob turned his head, winked and lit a cigar, exhaling a great wreath of tobacco smoke.

Wonder if he'll look so smug in a mindlink helmet, K'Raoda thought, seated across from Bob. Pouring himself a glass of water, he toasted McShane.

CHAPTER 16

THE HANDFUL OF Terrans strode purposefully down the gray, curving corridor of *Nasqa*. S'Cotar scuttled and flitted all about, paying them no mind.

"They're arrogant and literal-minded," POCSYM had said earlier, as the teaching helms settled over their heads. "Arrive undetected by their equipment and they'll think you're transmutes. You'll make it to the bridge."

When the helms lifted, three lost minutes later, they knew *Nasqa*: her layout, crew disposition, bridge operations; knew her as well as any S'Cotar. It was hard-won data, gleaned by POCSYM and Confederation Intelligence over the years.

The bridge crew should number no more than six. If the humans reached the bridge, they just might carry the day.

Maybe, thought John, running his thumb along the smooth leather of his holster.

POCSYM had put them as near to their objective as possible in so distant a moving target. They had only a walk of a hundred yards before the Terrans came to the bridge. S'Cotar came and went through the round, open doorway.

An alarm hooted. Lights flashed. Thinking it was all over, John turned to down the nearest aliens. But the S'Cotar ran past the humans, ignoring them. Giant blast doors began trundling shut. In a moment the bridge would be sealed.

"They're getting ready to engage *Implacable*," whispered Sutherland, drawing up beside John.

"Now or never," said John. "Let's go."

Caution tossed aside, he led the rush through the half-closed doors.

Nasqa's central screen showed the position of her fleet relative to two dots midpoint between Earth and Moon—*two* dots, John noted with relief. *Revenge* had joined *Implacable*.

High-backed chairs fronted the six bridge positions, hiding their occupants from view. "Turn slowly and you won't be hurt," lied John, seeking to spare only the consoles.

The chairs swiveled slowly about. Six empty chairs.

Drop your weapons or die where you stand, hissed something cold in all their minds.

The bridge swarmed with warriors.

K'Raoda had briefed McShane as the three of them rode the small, open hovercar through *Revenge*'s broad, empty corridors—more roadways than corridors—eerily still save for the vehicle's quiet purr.

"All we know of the mindslaves comes from POCSYM and N'Rar's *Annals of the Empire*," said the young officer. "Both say you must dominate the mindslaves, force them to your will."

He broke off, grabbing for a sidebar as D'Trelna banked sharply around a corner at full speed, yet another of Bob's cigars clenched between his teeth.

"Sorry," grunted the Captain. "You may not believe it, but I once fit into the cockpit of an esper fighter."

"Professor," continued the Tactics Officer, "you *must* overcome their initial resistance. It's imperative."

"And if I fail?"

D'Trelna spoke as K'Raoda hesitated. "They'll burn your cognitive centers out just to feel you twitch," he growled. "Don't fail."

They pulled up before a small door neatly lettered "Symbiotechnic Control Facility."

"Remember," added K'Raoda, "don't mindlink until POCSYM has us in orbit. And leave your communicator open on tactical. We'll be on the bridge, driving this battlewagon. You've got forty-five minutes to take control. Assuming our friends succeed aboard *Nasqa*, we'll need all the firepower you can give us. Good luck."

As soon as he was inside, they drove off.

An innocuous little room, thought Bob, to house something that excited so much horror.

Two thickly padded armchairs faced a soaring, blank screen—"primary battleboard," POCSYM had called it. Above each chair hung a translucent, bowl-shaped helmet, similar to POCSYM's teaching helms.

"Just sit in one of the chairs," POCSYM had instructed. "The helmet descends. What happens then varies each time. But you, not the mindslaves, must control events. And beware: they're treacherous."

The condemned man enjoyed a hearty last cigar, thought the academician, patting his pockets as he walked down the spiral staircase into the pit. Reaching the bottom, he groaned: D'Trelna had filched his last panatela. *C'est la guerre.* He smiled wistfully, recalling another war, other faces.

Bob wasn't long alone with his memories before D'Trelna called, "We're in space, Professor. Please begin."

"Tactical. Beginning now." He sank into one of the comfortable chairs, remembering, as the helmet lowered, to repeat "Tactical," keeping the channel open. The helmet settled down over his ears.

It began at once.

Hail, comrade, came a single, gentle whisper that was also many. *Welcome to our sepulcher. Long have we waited. What service may the penitent perform for Emperor and Empire?*

The Empire is dust, thought Bob. *You may, however, save all humanity from that which would destroy it.*

Surely a noble task, comrade, came the ghostly chorus. *We would know more, but sense that time is precious. Open your mind to us, that we may know all.*

Thank you, no. You've earned a durable reputation for malevolence.

One in which we take some pride, comrade.

There was a fierce buzzing, as of angry bees in conclave, then the attack Bob had expected struck.

Sharp stingers probed his mind's defenses, trying to win through. But the needles of raw mental energy couldn't penetrate, deflected by the professor's shield.

Oblivious to the hatred tearing at him, Bob was calmly reviewing Descartes's proofs for the existence of God.

"Tight little coffin," said John, looking about the tiny cell into which the Terrans were crammed, deep within *Nasqa*. The gray of the surrounding walls was broken only by the slight shimmer of the force field securing the doorway. A small, oval-shaped hole in the corner of the floor was the only amenity.

"They were expecting us," said Zahava after a moment's glum silence.

"How, though?" asked John, tentatively feeling the force field with his fingertips. The shimmer became a blur and he could move his hand no further. Giving up, he turned back to his companions.

"Maybe we triggered their intruder alert system after all," suggested Sutherland.

"They'd have cut us down as we arrived," John said. "No. Zahava's right—it was a trap, carefully laid. *Nasqa*'s crew had some lead time."

"Well, what now?" asked Bakunin. "They're probably going to interrogate us as they did your late President."

"We've got to escape—soon," said Zahava.

"Surely, André," Sutherland said, eyeing the Russian with a certain satisfaction, "the KGB must have a technique for breaking out of jail? Or do you just concern yourselves with keeping people in them?"

"Not my department, Bill," responded Bakunin with a negligent wave of his hand. "And a cheap shot, too, after all we've been through."

Their conversation was ended by the arrival of two warriors and a transmute. The doorway barrier vanished.

Come with us. The S'Cotar pointed their blasters at John, their leader motioning him away from the others with a flick of his pistol.

Silent till now, Greg elbowed his way past John. "We're all idiots," he said irritably, stepping in front of the leveled weapons. "We forgot about the warsuits—and so did they!"

With a shout, he threw himself on the aliens, dragging them down even as they fired.

"Take 'em!" barked John.

It was short and messy, the humans kicking and gouging for the eyes, the insectoids fighting back with tentacles and mandibles, Zahava ending it with a captured blaster.

The victors stood, a collection of bruises and cuts. All but Greg. The lanky geologist lay unmoving between two of the enemy dead. Gently turning him, John saw why: most of Greg's stomach was gone. His warsuit had failed, as he must have known it would, beneath the close fire of several weapons.

John gently closed his friend's sightless eyes and stood, face grim and set. "I say we still have time to take the bridge. Agreed?"

From somewhere deep within Descartes, McShane half noticed the mindslaves' attack waning, the once-sharp buzzing now muted. Distant but distinct, a voice called his name.

"D'Trelna to McShane. S'Cotar forward elements are coming within range. See if you can activate the Weapons systems. Bridge monitors still show them down."

With a small mental sigh, Bob carefully shelved Descartes, then called, *Brothers, sisters, I call upon you to right ancient wrongs.*

The buzzing stopped.

I exhort you by the names of all those whom you condemned to your fate, right the wrong you've done. Destroy the enemy now before you.

The whisper that was one-yet-many sounded again.

Bob pondered his reply.

Yes, he finally answered. *I promise. Help us now and it shall be done.*

When?

When the enemy is destroyed.

It is agreed.

The battleboard came alive, transformed into a three-dimensional projection of the solar system. The advancing S'Cotar were now well inside the orbit of Mars, deployed in a great wedge pointed straight at Earth.

They are within our range, comrade. You have but to give the command.

He spoke it aloud. "Fire."

The Terrans had almost reached *Nasqa*'s bridge when the alarm sounded, this time for them.

Not that the four could hear it. A passing group of warriors whirled and fired. Thanks to the warsuits and Zahava's vigilance, the insectoids died in the exchange, not the humans.

Then it was a desperate, running battle the rest of the way to the bridge. John leading, they weaved through a maze of corridors, blasting down the enemy before them, keeping those behind at bay.

A mixed party of warriors and transmutes guarded the bridge, weapons ready. They opened fire just as John and Zahava lobbed the small spheroids taken from their utility belts.

A pulsating red glow filled the corridor. Blaster fire crackled from both sides.

The aliens died, their aim distorted by spectral grenades keyed to their vision. But the bridge was sealed.

Undeterred, John and Zahava busied themselves before the massive doors. Sutherland and Bakunin kept their pursuers back.

"Hug the wall!" John ordered. They braced themselves against the bridge's bulkhead as Zahava pressed a button on her belt.

The huge blast doors didn't so much blow up as disintegrate in a fierce white heat, frames buckling.

The Terrans charged in and killed the deck crew.

"Gentlemen, if you'd guard our rear," John asked, and Bakunin and Sutherland ran out again.

Going to the communications console, John tapped withdrawal orders into *Nasqa*'s computer. He and Zahava watched as, a moment later, the S'Cotar fleet began obediently dispersing.

"Time to leave, I think." Bill's voice was tense over the commnet. "Lots of company." He and the Russian dived through the doorway, energy bolts rending the air above them. Crouching to either side of the door, they fired back.

"POCSYM, pull us out in one minute," John ordered.

"Acknowledged."

He ran to the command console, pressed an isolated button, then shot a finger at Zahava, standing by the XO's station. She carefully typed a few characters, using keys never meant for human digits, then nodded at John.

A great bolt of raw, red energy tore through the navigation console, ochre flame and blue sparks exploding in its wake.

"Heavy weapons!" Zahava turned toward the door as a solid wave of S'Cotar swarmed the bridge, overrunning Sutherland and Bakunin.

"Now, POCSYM!" shouted John, blasting two warriors and grappling with another.

Battered, singed and exhausted, four Terrans stood on *Implacable*'s bridge.

CHAPTER 17

A TRANSPARENT BLISTER atop the great ship, *Revenge*'s bridge was the size of *Implacable*'s Hangar Deck. D'Trelna found its cavernous, many-tiered vastness even eerier than the still, dead corridors he'd just traversed, conveying McShane to the mind-slaves.

Only ten of *Implacable*'s crew could be spared to man the mindslaver and they were scattered, effectively swallowed by the huge bridge.

Despite having done it before, the Captain took the command chair, center of the fifth and highest level, with great reluctance. T'Nil had sat in that chair, and S'Tar and Q'Nor—the legendary Emperors of the Second Dynasty, men whose sagas were inseparably interwoven with the rich tapestry of Empire.

"You may lift ship, POCSYM," he said quietly.

After fifty centuries, T'Nil's *Revenge* was spaceborn again.

"All systems except Weapons operational," reported K'Raoda from the XO's station, next to the Captain's. "We don't enjoy the degree of maneuverability we would with a full crew, but we can move."

"We don't need her for more than an orbital fort," said D'Trelna.

"Is that *Implacable*?" he asked, looking up to his right. A silver ship made tiny by distance hung there.

"Sure is," confirmed the young officer. "I'd know that old hulk anywhere." His eyes returned to his console. It was a marvel, infinitely more sophisticated than anything aboard *Implacable*.

116

"Speak with respect, Subcommander," said D'Trelna softly, still looking up. "She's the best ever made without brainstrip technology. She's fast and she's clean—unlike this wondrous horror." He dropped his gaze, gesturing about the still, shadowy bridge.

The two men retreated into silence.

It only seems a long time, D'Trelna reassured himself, watching the S'Cotar fleet on his screen. It really hadn't been that long since the assault team left—untrained friends sent against the mother ship of a cruel and crafty foe.

Nor that long since he'd sent McShane alone into that metallic shaft of a room, an old man pitted against five millennia of intelligent, festering malevolence.

It has too been a long time, fat man, sneered a voice deep within him. *A long time. They're dead. And you've lost. You should have run while you could, but no, the hero of T'Qar doesn't run. He—*

As he squelched the voice, everything broke.

"*Nasqa* party returned. Mission accomplished," reported an elated L'Wrona from *Implacable.*

A dot in the center of the enemy fleet projection winked out. A new and distant sun flared briefly in the direction of the now-scattering S'Cotar, then vanished forever.

"Hang on to your chinstraps up there," said a tired voice on the commnet. McShane's voice.

"We've lost the helm, Captain." Alarmed, K'Raoda pressed a series of unresponsive controls.

"Shield's up," called a familiar voice. "Weapons systems arming."

"What's the effective range of an Imperial mindslaver, K'Raoda?" asked the Captain, unperturbed.

"No idea, sir." The Tactics Officer gave up on the console, turning to face D'Trelna. "The *Annals* tiptoe around a lot of this."

"I think we're about to find out." He looked up at the waves of sleek, deadly missiles pouring away from them.

You must help us. The sibilant whisper came again into Bob's mind. *But it's never really left,* he thought tiredly. *How?*

Join your mind with ours. The enemy is many. Only with your help can we prevail.

Hesitantly, Bob sent out a tentative tendril of thought.

Something dark and strong coiled around it, pulling the rest of him into a swirling vortex of white-hot hate. Before he could feel more than a twinge of terror, the vortex coalesced into a surging river of incandescence. The river became thousands of raging streams, each pushing a small, cold point of light toward a larger one.

Bob was one burning stream. He was all streams. A lifetime's hostility, sublimated to the dictates of civilization, was being called forth.

Seen from *Revenge*, the new suns lived just long enough to become a great fireball, then died. The mindslaves had kept their word.

"Gods of our fathers!" exclaimed L'Wrona from *Implacable*'s command chair as an ensign deactivated series after series of dead sensors. "What was in those warheads?" he asked over the commnet.

"Maybe we could pry one open," suggested K'Raoda, looking out through *Revenge*'s again transparent dome. It had opaqued in instant response to the blinding light, clearing just as quickly once the danger passed.

"Maybe we won't," grumbled D'Trelna.

"Did you track those missiles, L'Wrona?" he asked. "The detectors here are still a mystery."

"We couldn't, Captain. They vanished a few seconds after launch."

"Check your hyperspace gear on point one-one-zero scale."

"They went into hyperdrive!" came the startled response. "But hyperdrives aren't that small—why, even the Imperials—"

K'Raoda broke in excitedly. "The mindslaves! It must be! Somehow they can hurl weapons through hyperspace and drop them on target. But those detonations? What's in those warheads?"

"Minute quantities of matter/antimatter, held in stasis." POCSYM spoke for the first time in hours. "The stasis field is released when the weapons arrive on target. You've just witnessed the result."

A low, keening moan interrupted them.

The Captain rose. "Professor, can you hear me?" he called anxiously.

Another moan was the only response.

"K'Raoda, you have the con. Medtech Q'Nil with me." D'Trelna made for the door. A slight figure detached itself from a chair two tiers down, scrambling up an access ladder to join the officer, medkit strapped across from a holstered blaster.

Bob broke free of the ebbing stream. Or was shoved from it, he could never remember.

His next recollection was of something shining—the helmet? lifting away from him. Then an all-consuming pain invaded his skull.

"They're eating my brain!" he cried, or so D'Trelna later swore.

Q'Nil was sure the Captain would kill them, racing the hovercar around sharp corners at full speed, recklessly banking and swerving.

They were at the mindslave chamber in minutes, D'Trelna charging through the door and down the stairs to kneel over Bob. The Terran lay stretched out on the floor, ominously still, his breathing shallow. He opened his eyes, blinking weakly as Q'Nil examined him.

"Captain," he managed to croak. "Captain. The mind-slaves . . . you must kill them. My word . . . agreed to help us . . . let them die."

D'Trelna blinked, then avoided the injured man's piercing gaze. "Well?" he asked as Q'Nil administered a hypo.

"Shock, fever, exhaustion. I've given him a sedative. He'll need lots of rest, but barring complications he should be all right."

"Captain," Bob whispered hoarsely. Seizing D'Trelna's tunic with both hands, he pulled the K'Ronarin's face to within inches of his own. "Your word!"

"I can't!" cried the officer, pulling away. He stood, his face set. "You did a great and wondrous thing, my friend. But you exceeded your authority when you made that promise. Hell, man, you exceeded mine! Without those brainstrips, *Revenge* is just another toothless relic. And we may still need her.''

"If you could only have felt their anguish—and the terrible catharsis that's their only pleasure, J'Quel,'' said Bob, rallying voice and mind for a final plea. ''They desire only oblivion—deserve it as a mercy!''

"You're suggesting, Bob,'' came the gentle rejoinder, ''that we can only save those brainstrips—legally centuries dead, their names forgotten—we can only save these dead things by killing them.''

He bent down and lifted one of McShane's arms. ''Help me get him to sick bay, Q'Nil. He's delirious.''

CHAPTER 18

"THIS MAN"—Admiral L'Guan beamed, draping an affectionate arm about D'Trelna's broad shoulders—"once led me such a wild chase through an uncharted asteroid belt that I marvel to be alive." Chuckling, he slipped his arm away to hook a drink from a passing steward.

The K'Ronarin fleet had shown up eight days after the S'Cotar's destruction. Standing well off Terra, its senior officers had flitted down—via POCSYM—to a series of meetings with the heads of all but one of Earth's most powerful nations. Although ignoring its invitation, the Soviet Union had sent a freshly debriefed Andreyev Bakunin to the conference as an observer, a continuing status he now shared aboard *Vigilant* with the two Americans and the Israeli, also just returned from home.

The meetings, held on a secluded ranch in the high desert of New Mexico, had been cordial, reinforcing the existing groundwork of mutual trust. The K'Ronarin Ambassador, once he arrived, would find the Terrans receptive to a mutual aid pact.

L'Guan was every inch the professional soldier-diplomat: tall, handsome, with silver-streaked hair and aquiline features, he stood resplendent in a bemedaled, jet-black dress uniform, a gracious, charming host to the Terrans and K'Ronarins thronging *Vigilant*'s spacious reception hall.

"You *really* couldn't catch me?" asked *Implacable*'s skipper disbelievingly. "I thought you were toying with me!" Both burst into laughter.

"Maneuvers?" asked John, sipping his drink.

"Maneuvers? This old pirate? Ha!" the Admiral laughed. "He was a smuggler, running—what was it that time, J'Quel, null-grav spices?"

"No, sir. Surface-to-space missile parts for the colonists on Q'Tul Seven. As you'll recall, Admiral, our myopic policy was to close our eyes and pretend that the S'Cotar would just—"

"As you can see," interrupted L'Guan good-humoredly, "we've had our differences. When the entire Confederation finally came around to J'Quel's way of thinking, he came in one day and offered his services. It was because of his . . . ah . . . unusual background and subsequent record that I chose him to lead this expedition.

"You signed up when, Captain, six years ago?" he asked, draining his glass. A crewman whisked it away.

"Yes, sir. Just after the debacle of U'Tria Nine. And a difficult six years it's been, Admiral," continued D'Trelna. He reminded Zahava of a pugnacious bulldog that had once hung around her apartment building, terrifying the neighborhood kids.

"Oh, I think we have them now, Captain," said the senior officer, exuding a quiet confidence. "Or rather, they no longer have us, thanks to all of you." His gaze swept the circle of his listeners: John, Zahava, Montanoya, Sutherland and Bakunin, the last of whom wore the dress uniform of a KGB colonel. "Our forces are already reoccupying the sectors they've pulled out of."

Sutherland, dressed in the Outfit's uniform—two-piece designer suit, hand-finished white shirt, silk tie and Swiss cordovans—raised his glass, saluting L'Guan. "I'd like to thank you, sir, for a grand reception, and for my being the first Terran to enjoy a manhattan in Earth orbit."

The Admiral gave a slight bow, then added mischievously, "Actually, someone from your country's diplomatic corps claimed that record over an hour ago." He glanced about the room. "Hmm. He seems to have gone off with one of the women of my bridge crew. Busy setting another new record, no doubt."

Zahava, earlier unrecognized by Bill in a lavender Dior gown, turned to Montanoya. "How did you convince all these people to come, José?" she asked. Her long-stemmed crystal wineglass swept over the gathering.

The hall thronged with military and civilians, K'Ronarin and Terran, all in after-dinner attire and wearing translators. The U.S. Marine Corps chamber orchestra, smartly set off in mess whites, was playing Bach. The Earth hung seemingly just beyond the transparent far wall, a green, brown and blue orb broken by swirling mists of white.

"I wish I could say it was my diplomatic skill," replied Montanoya, his own eyes taking in the reception. "Credit where it's due, though. The recent ground, air and space actions lit up battleboards around the planet like a Christmas tree.

"They probably didn't tell you, Admiral, but several idiots wanted to start lobbing nukes at both K'Ronarin and S'Cotar fleets. But when the morons saw the numbers and weaponry involved, cooler heads were able to prevail. Fortunately, one of those heads belonged to our then-Vice President, Pete Martin."

He stopped to light a cigar, first delicately biting the tip off and swallowing it.

"You've stunned the world into at least a temporary peace," he continued, exhaling a great wreath of smoke. "Hostilities of any sort have ceased in most areas of the globe. It's as if the world were holding its collective breath, waiting to see if you're going to conquer us, lend technical aid or ask for colonization rights."

He smiled at L'Guan's startled expression. "My summation of yesterday's Situation Report from our State Department."

"Surely the masses know nothing of this?" asked Bakunin with a tinge of alarm.

"The 'masses,'" said Montanoya, slowly hissing the s's, "know nothing, Colonel. You can rest assured—for now."

The Russian's bourbon and spring water stopped halfway to his lips. "Surely sir, you—the United States—don't intend to unilaterally reveal all of this to an unprepared world!"

"Maybe your half aren't prepared, Colonel"—the National Security Advisor smiled thinly—"but ours is. So are the Chinese. And with a neo-populist instead of a plutocrat in the White House, look for that announcement to come soon—and forcefully.

"You may have to give up the Black Sea *dasha*, Colonel."

"Actually, Zahava," he said, turning back to the Israeli, "I had to turn people away from this reception to cull down to the hundred or so *Vigilant* could accommodate. You'd think more people would have sense enough not to let a computer scatter their atoms across space." More smoke billowed toward the transparent bubble that was the ceiling.

"Good evening, Admiral, Captain, everyone," spoke an assured voice.

They turned to greet L'Wrona. A black-clad commando officer, about L'Wrona's age but taller, was with him. Both wore duty uniforms with sidearms.

"Subcommander N'Tal V'Arta, Fleet Commando," said L'Wrona, introducing him. "My second cousin."

L'Guan nodded at V'Arta, then turned to L'Wrona. "How stands the Fleet, Commander My-Lord-Captain L'Wrona?" he asked cheerfully of the Watch Officer.

"All quiet, sir. Nice party." He nodded, listening for a moment to the strings. "Different music, but very, very nice.

"We just looked in on our patient," he continued, referring to McShane. "He's quite chipper. Fleet Surgeon says he can rejoin us tomorrow."

"Just as well," said John. "He was threatening to break out of there."

"You don't have to tell us," said *Implacable*'s XO with a smile. "We caught him prowling the reaction force ready room on Six Deck. Had to haul him back to sick bay.

"We'd best get back to the bridge. Good evening all, Admiral, Captain."

L'Wrona and V'Arta melted into the crowd.

"And I musn't neglect my other guests," said L'Guan. "You'll excuse me?"

He wasn't gone more than a few seconds before Harrison turned to D'Trelna. "'Commander My-Lord-Captain L'Wrona'?" he asked, cocking an eyebrow.

"Ah, yes." The Captain sighed. "The Admiral is an Imperial. Ancient titles are important to that faction. They'd like more of them.''

He flagged down a steward—they were less attentive with the Admiral gone—relieving the man of an entire platter of luscious-looking meat canapés. ''My First Officer is heir to a great tradition,'' he said between munches. '''Lord-Captain of the Imperial Guard, Defender of the Outer Marches, Margrave of U'Tria.'

''The titles are mostly courtesy. The last Imperial Guardsmen fell millennia ago, the Outer Marches haven't been heard from since POCSYM bid his creators farewell and the attack on U'Tria Nine—L'Wrona's home—precipitated this war.

''Care for a canapé?'' he offered, passing the plate toward his friends.

''You ate them all,'' said Bakunin bluntly, thrusting it back. ''Oh.''

D'Trelna put the platter on a table. ''The titles convey the right to lead the Fleet Commando, if it ever should fight as a unit again. The Commando traces its origins back to T'Nil's Task Force Forty-Seven Marines—the unit that seized Imperial Communications and later formed the core of his own guard.

''But the war's just about over. I doubt L'Wrona will get to exercise his birthright.''

Admiral L'Guan reappeared. Slipping up to D'Trelna, he whispered urgently in the other's ear, walking quickly away even as the Captain nodded.

''Duty calls.'' D'Trelna sighed, putting down his glass and stepping toward the arched entrance way.

''Seems to be calling others, too,'' said John. They all followed his gaze. A steady trickle of K'Ronarin officers were exiting as unobtrusively as possible, their departure sparked by a hurried whisper from L'Guan.

''Captain, we're almost family,'' John said with a hurt look. ''Level with us.''

''Really. I can't.'' He looked embarrassed.

''Afraid you'll frighten the natives, J'Quel?'' asked Sutherland, smiling sympathetically.

''All right. Come with me. I'll explain outside.'' They

passed a mixed group of European and Asian diplomats listening attentively to a crimson-uniformed Survey officer.

Gaining the corridor, D'Trelna broke into a brisk trot. Startled, the others ran after him.

"*Revenge*'s watch crew just signaled 'Intruder Alert,'" he explained hurriedly. "We're assembling a force on the Hangar Deck. POCSYM will transport."

In five minutes they were on the Hangar Deck. Some of the hastily gathered commandos were still fastening their warsuits when L'Guan ordered POCSYM to "Transport!"

The Terrans never knew if they'd been included because of design or haste. Regardless, they faced *Revenge*'s surprised bridge crew with two dozen *Vigilant* commandos.

"Not here, Captain!" K'Raoda called urgently from the command tier. "The mindslave area!"

D'Trelna cursed. "How many S'Cotar?" he demanded.

"I don't know, sir. Fleet hasn't installed S'Cotar detectors yet. We just sealed the bridge and called for help."

"POCSYM," the Captain snarled into his communicator. "Think you can get us to the right coordinates this time?"

They were in the corridor outside the now-sealed door of the mindslave room. Only D'Trelna had been there before.

"No time to burn our way in," he grumbled. "They're probably after the brainpods. Kill the mindslaves and this ship's just so much scrap metal.

"Pass me a blastpack."

Motioning everyone back, the Captain placed the charge. Setting the timer, he ran to join them behind the corridor's sheltering curve.

"Temperature in brainpods rising into critical," reported K'Raoda, worriedly eyeing a bridge monitor. "They must be using a semi."

The explosion preempted any response.

D'Trelna charged through the still-glowing doorway, pistol at the ready. He froze at the railing, looking down into the room, stunned. The commandos halted behind him.

"Are you crazy, man?" he shouted, bounding down the stairs and knocking a big semiportable blaster from McShane's hands. The weapon had gouged a hole deep into the nearly seamless access hatch set in the rear bulkhead.

The older man stood mute, staring at the wall. John and Zahava made their way through the commandos to his side.

"Bob," said John softly, laying a gentle hand on his mentor's shoulder.

"I gave my word." McShane finally looked at them. "My only regret, Captain, is that I failed." His eyes bored into D'Trelna's own. "It's wrong and you know it."

The Captain averted his eyes. "Look . . ."

"Don't tell me you need this ship, J'Quel," said McShane. "You've wiped out the main S'Cotar force—your own Intelligence says so. Once you find their home world, you can mop up with your regular forces."

"Bob, I—"

"How do we differ from the S'Cotar, J'Quel?"

Caught off guard, the K'Ronarin stumbled. "Well why, why we're human, of course."

"Isn't it rather the *attributes* of our humanity—love, compassion, mercy—which distinguish us from other intelligences, Captain?"

"Professor, I must insist that you—"

"How then, Captain," pressed McShane coldly, "how then are we human if we enshrine hatred, eschew compassion and remain merciless in the face of such unmitigated suffering as is here?" He jerked a thumb at the brainpod area. "Tell me, J'Quel," he asked quietly. "I'm listening."

"Magnificent," breathed Sutherland, high atop the stairs.

"POCSYM," said D'Trelna, "transport Mr. McShane back to *Vigilant*'s sick bay. Me as well. Return the rest of our force to *Vigilant*'s Hangar Deck."

A few hours later, while McShane was under close guard, someone who knew how to use a blastpack—L'Guan was never able to find out who—finished the job, commuting the mindslaves' sentence of eternal torment to one of sweet oblivion.

John and Zahava had a suspect, though. Confronted with his name months later, McShane would only smile inscrutably and say, "The triumph of decency over duty is a rare and glorious thing."

CHAPTER 19

"WHEN YOU ASKED for this meeting, Captain," said Admiral L'Guan, looking severely at D'Trelna. "I wasn't aware that Professor McShane would be present."

Bob, much his old self, sat between Zahava and John. Across the table, D'Trelna and L'Wrona flanked their Admiral, facing the Terrans.

"Fleet Surgeon has certified Professor McShane as recovered, sir, and his unfortunate actions aboard *Revenge* the result of stress." The Captain met his superior's hard stare with one of pure innocence.

"And," he continued before the Admiral could press him, "it's because of Bob—Professor McShane's experience with the mindslaves that we're here."

"Really?" drawled L'Guan, raising an eyebrow, unconvinced.

"As the . . . ah, 'brainstrips'"—Bob lingered distastefully over the word—"used my mind, Admiral, so, it seems did I use theirs." His voice had regained its vibrancy.

"In some way the melding of my mind with theirs lent me a heightened mental acuity. I saw new interrelations—new possibilities—things which escaped me before."

"Such as?"

"Such as this war is not over. Your fleet and my planet may yet be in grave danger."

"Specifics, please," demanded L'Guan tensely, eyes searching for clues in Bob's impassive face.

"Lying in your wondrous sick bay, Admiral, I kept going

over the events of the past weeks. Especially the part played in them by humanity's benevolent savant, POCSYM Six.''

McShane paused, hands patting his empty shirt pockets. D'Trelna passed the professor a cigar and lit it. Bob grunted his thanks. Puffing, he leaned back. '' *'Essentia non sunt multiplicanda praeter necessitatum*,' Admiral,'' he continued expansively.

''We turned in the translators last week, Bob,'' reminded Zahava gently.

''Sorry. 'Fact need not be multiplied beyond necessity.' Or so said William of Ockham some time ago. We've taken his statement as one of the basic axioms of rationality—dubbed it 'Ockham's Razor.' ''

''Fascinating, Mr McShane,'' L'Guan said with mild sarcasm, his patience slipping. ''But how does this apply—''

''POCSYM has weaved a tangled web of deceit. Rather than facts, he's multiplied lies beyond necessity. And like all liars, he's become ensnared in his own web. Listen to me.'' He held up a hand as L'Guan looked ready to interrupt.

''One. By his own account POCSYM was able to scan *Implacable*, identify her crew as K'Ronarin and place us aboard her in the vicinity of Mars. Yet this same entity was unable to detect one small shipload of aliens who then landed on Earth unopposed and established their base.

''Two. He's told us that the S'Cotar wanted very badly to capture Earth. Why? Not for the planet itself, but because of POCSYM. Yet, again by his own admission, POCSYM's only unusual ability is that of molecular transport—a capability the S'Cotar have through telekinesis. Why not just drop a planet-buster or biophage us?

''Three. POCSYM delayed coming to the aid of *Implacable*'s ground force. Why? Because, he assured us, his systems had been largely inactive for centuries. Systems which had not more than hours before transported us safely to *Implacable*—a complex operation surely requiring more than a few nonsomnolent circuits.

''I'm sure you can each think of other examples—the raid on *Nasqa*, for example. But that's enough for me,'' McShane concluded, leaning back in his chair. "POCSYM's hiding something. And we'd better find out what before it kills us."

"Circumstantial evidence, Professor," said L'Guan after a moment, visibly relaxing. "POCSYM is very complex—almost human. And very, very old. You've got to expect inconsistencies."

"Inconsistencies certainly, sir," said D'Trelna, picking up the argument. "But not demonstrable falsehoods."

John couldn't recall *Implacable*'s Captain ever being so well turned out, not even for the reception. His boots shone, his pants and shirt were clean and pressed, campaign ribbons, battlestars and two valor medals hung over and from his right breast pocket. He still wore the regulation long-barreled blaster, but the butt was inlaid with semiprecious stones and nestled in a gleaming black leather holster.

"'Demonstrable falsehoods'?" repeated the Admiral slowly, frowning.

"I've had Subcommander K'Raoda checking POCSYM's bonafides, sir, using *Revenge*'s memory cells."

"And?"

"All references to the POCSYM series require special access codes—codes which may be in Archives but certainly aren't with the Fleet. K'Raoda reports that any attempt to bypass the authentication system would scrub the needed data."

"So?" The Admiral shrugged. "Naturally, information concerning a matter transport system would be guarded."

"Yes, sir. But the reference to POCSYM wasn't found under 'Matter Transport.'"

"Oh? Under what, then?"

"'Biofab.'"

There was a long silence. Then the Admiral rose and walked to the armor-glass wall. He stood for a moment, hands clasped behind his back, looking out on a small part of his fleet and the blue world below. Starlight gleamed off the twin comets of his rank, set on his collar.

Turning back toward the table, his lips were pursed, his face thoughtful. "An intact Imperial transport system. A functioning—until recently—mindslaver dreadnought. And now a reference to biofabs. Why is it that we're suddenly, after all these centuries, confronted with every technological excess of the late Empire? Why in this one star system? Speculation, anyone?''

"What is a biofab?" asked John.

"Biofabs," L'Guan said, "were another marvel of the Empire—products of genetic engineering created by a rebel sector to aid its secession. The ultimate product of biological fabrication—hence the term—was a superman: long-lived, resilient, aggressive, each one a genius.

"The traitorous sector governor who created them formed these biofabs into elite shock troops—they'd have eaten our commandos alive—and had them crew her fleet. Can you guess the result?''

"They took over?'' speculated the Israeli.

"With a vengeance." The Admiral nodded. "Sterilized half the planets in that sector. Biophaged them to eliminate the inferior species—us—cluttering them. There were exceptions, though. A small number of people were spared to serve the biofabs—as mindslaves.

"It took a decade and fleets of the *Revenge* class to exterminate that plague. As you might guess, there were and still are rather drastic penalties for performing biofab research.''

He turned back to the others. "No speculation?''

"Not enough parts of the puzzle fit yet, Admiral," said John. "But K'Raoda has an unpleasant fact for you.''

"As you're aware, sir," the young officer said, "POCSYM has stated that his main installation is beneath the Isle of Manhattan, under one of the largest Terran cities." He paused for effect. "Not true.''

"What?! But I've been there. We all have!''

"You *were* in the central facility, sir," continued K'Raoda, unruffled. "You were *not*, as were none of us, beneath Manhattan. In fact, you weren't even on Terra.''

The Admiral sat silently, beyond surprise.

"Recall, if you would, sir, that only POCSYM would normally know where we were if transported to an unfamiliar location. That's how the ruse is accomplished.''

"Can you prove this, K'Raoda?''

"Yes, sir. *Revenge* has subterranean detectors far superior to our own. Analysis of the area below Manhattan revealed nothing but planetary crust all the way down to the magma."

"Then where *is* our faithful servant?" asked L'Guan.

"There." They followed where K'Raoda's finger pointed, through the armor glass, at the moon, just beginning its climb from behind the Earth's curve. "Grid eighty-one, Terran reference 'The Lake of Dreams.' Its interior is sensor-blanked by Imperial-grade technology. Analysis of the energy pattern protecting that area shows it to be a larger model of *Revenge*'s shield—the matrixes are identical. Seems POCSYM doesn't want us to look at something."

"How do you know it's POCSYM?" challenged L'Guan.

"At the Captain's request, sir, I had POCSYM transport me back to his operations area, ostensibly to ensure that all of *Implacable*'s equipment had been returned to the ship. Actually, to try to trace where I was taken."

"Was this effort successful, Captain D'Trelna?"

"It was, Admiral. Using a low-powered snooperbeam, we followed an energy trace directly to a point in that lunar shield. The point breached for a nanosecond under the impetus of a surge."

"Were you able to get any life form readings through the breach?"

"S'Cotar. Several miles distant but numerous."

The Admiral's expression was impassive as he spoke into his communicator. "Captain S'Nar. 'Fleet Alert,' please. Emphasize it's not a drill. Then plot a bombardment pattern for the Terran satellite—get the coordinates from L'Wrona on *Implacable*." He'd hardly finished before the battle klaxon sounded.

"One further revelation before we adjourn, sir," said McShane, holding up a hand as L'Guan rose. The Admiral sank back into his chair.

"I don't know if I can take any more," he said with a weak grin. "What?"

"We believe we've found the S'Cotar home system," D'Trelna said. The outside view blurred as *Vigilant*'s shield went from meteor to battle force.

"Where?" snapped the Admiral, leaning forward.

"Here."

The Captain pressed on before his superior could recover.

"We've been using drones from *Revenge* for picket duty, searching for any concentrations of S'Cotar that might have escaped."

"I know," said L'Guan, his voice made too loud by the sudden silencing of the klaxon. "So?"

"They have sophisticated detectors, sir. The asteroid belt shows signs of extensive mining, over a long time and only recently abandoned."

"Mined for how long, Captain?"

"At least several centuries. Many of the larger asteroids are hollow, and life readings indicate the presence of vast numbers of S'Cotar. We also have grave suspicions, as yet unconfirmed, about five of the satellites of Saturn.

"Happily, we seem to have accounted for all but a handful of their ships."

CHAPTER 20

"No!" CRIED ZAHAVA. "Admiral, your weapons could alter the moon's orbit. Do that and you'd kill millions on Earth. Tidal waves, earthquakes—the whole isostatic condition of the planet would be disrupted!"

L'Guan had been about to order heavy bombardment of the fragile lunar surface.

"She's right," said McShane earnestly. "Earth and moon dance a delicate ballet, sir. To tamper with one is to tamper with the other." L'Guan looked at him solemnly. "You see, gravity, Admiral, is the stuff that holds all of this to—"

D'Trelna loudly cleared his throat. "The Admiral is a master astrophysicist."

L'Guan held up his hand. "POCSYM is in league with our deadliest enemies. It isn't necessary for me to solve the mystery of it, merely to resolve it. Now. The only other option I have is ground assault on a hardened fortress, an action that would cost the lives of many of my men and probably not succeed. And if we don't take that fortress out, no matter what the cost, then Terra has an enemy camped on her doorstep. And K'Ronar has one at her back."

He slapped the table. "We have to do it now!"

"Sir, there is another possibility," Harrison said, glancing at D'Trelna. "We'd like your permission to try an appeal to logic and first principles." D'Trelna nodded. "If that fails, *then* ring down the heavens."

"Good morning, POCSYM," said John.

"Good morning, gentlemen." The rich voice echoed through the machine's great central chamber.

John and the Captain stood on a small service catwalk spanning POCSYM's main shaft. Miles below and above, disappearing into a fine pinpoint of light, the endless array of equipment encircled the brilliantly lit tunnel. Small maintenance robots went silently about their housekeeping chores. A dry, warm breeze caressed the men's faces.

"You asked, literally, to see me, gentlemen. This will have to do—I'm not very compact. How may I help you?"

As John leaned against the rail, D'Trelna unfolded a paper, cleared his throat and began reading. "By order of Grand Admiral L'Guan and subject to confirmation by the Confederation Council, be it known that Planetary Operations Control System, Mode Six, programmed by Imperial Colonial Command on K'Ronar, Imperium 2028, and now operating at"—here followed a long series of star coordinates—"and known by the acronym 'POCSYM Six,' is granted sentient being status within the definition of sentience as promulgated by the Seventh Confederation Council.

"If you accept, POCSYM," added the Captain, "this automatically confers citizenship, retroactive to Compact that established the Confederation. Do you accept?" He returned the paper to his pocket.

"Yes, thank you, Captain. A very touching gesture. Please extend my deep appreciation to the Admiral."

Not pausing, D'Trelna took another document from his tunic. "Citizen POCSYM Six," he intoned, "be advised that I am a sworn officer of the K'Ronarin Confederation, and that I hold a warrant for your arrest issued under Fleet Articles of War.

"Do you submit yourself to arrest, Citizen POCSYM Six?"

"That was very clever, Captain," said POCSYM after a moment. "I sense Mr. Harrison's fine Medician hand in this. By accepting citizenship, I granted your Confederation jurisdiction over me.

"Is this a test of my loyalty, my logic, my sanity, perhaps? Do you hope to sway me from my purpose by sweet reason?"

"Do you submit yourself to arrest?" repeated D'Trelna.

"What are the charges? Littering?"

"High treason. Lending aid and comfort to the enemy."

There was a long silence. Then a different voice. Dry, crisp, efficient.

"You've gone far, Captain. My compliments. But not quite far enough. You see, I *am* the enemy."

A S'Cotar stood on the catwalk.

"How many intelligent life forms do you think the Empire found in our galaxy, gentlemen?" POCSYM continued, ignoring the alien.

"None that I'm aware of," replied an impassive D'Trelna. "And we've found only the S'Cotar."

Warily eyeing the transmute, John shifted away from the railing, ready for action.

"More precisely, Captain, the S'Cotar found you, didn't they, ten Earth years ago?

"But yes, we, the Empire of which I am the last survivor, also found no others. The galaxy is empty, save for hundreds of ruined worlds, thousands of cities, all slag-heaps, their radioactivity long dissipated. Many worlds bring forth intelligent life. Few races, though, survive their adolescence—nuclear fission is a deadly toy. K'Ronar, with its atomics restricted to a small technoaristocracy, was a survivor. We found only the remains of others, long dead. We were alone."

"Aren't you forgetting someone, POCSYM?" asked John. "What about Terra?"

"I thought it clear, Mr. Harrison. You're undoubtedly of K'Ronarin stock. Early in the Empire's bloody history, more than one wave of refugees fled into uncharted space. Few were ever heard from again. By the time the first Imperial scouts reached this sector, the colonists had sunk to barbarism. We put you back on the road to civilization and your birthright, the universe. You're as much K'Ronarin and owe as much to the Empire as does the Captain."

"How is this relevant to your dramatic statement of a moment ago?" asked D'Trelna.

"The Empire did not discover the S'Cotar. Through me, it created them."

"Biofabs!"

"Ah, you've been doing your homework. Good. Yes, the S'Cotar are my biological fabrications."

"Biofab research has been proscribed since the Second Interregnum, ending the Biofab Wars," said D'Trelna. "That was an Imperial edict, POCSYM, which you've chosen to ignore. Why?"

"Captain, I can only exercise free will within the bounds of my master program. One of its principal tenets was the construction and deployment of these biofabs, the S'Cotar."

"Biofabs *are* clones, aren't they?" asked Harrison.

No, said a cold whisper in their heads. *We are as unique as you. POCSYM created one thousand three hundred and eighty-nine original and distinct S'Cotar two centuries ago. They then bred their own larvae. A society planned to the last detail awaited them. No thrashing about, no civil wars. We are one.*

"God," said John in disgust.

"You've met Gaun-Sharick, I believe," said POCSYM. "Gaun has, among other things, headed my efforts to keep the Terrans from stumbling over the old temple-transporter sites, with occasionally unpleasant consequences.

"Gaun, perhaps our guests find your physiognomy distressing."

Cindy stood there, wearing a yellow halter top, faded denim cutoffs and a pair of sandals. "Better?" it asked with a freckle-faced smile and a toss of the head. The long flaxen hair swished back over a bare, tanned shoulder.

"Worse," gritted John.

Fred Langston took Cindy's place with the same slight ripple that had heralded the girl-form's appearance. It puffed a meerschaum pipe, hands in the tweed jacket pockets, Gucci-shod feet crossed as it leaned insouciantly against the railing.

"Why?" demanded D'Trelna.

"Why what, Captain?" asked POCSYM, puzzled.

"Why this entire exercise, POCSYM!" D'Trelna's face grew dark with rage. "Why create these monstrosities—telepathic monstrosities at that?" He stabbed a finger at the Langston-thing. "Why have them descend on us, kill millions of our people, and alter our very way of life?"

"For your own good, that's why," said the unperturbed

voice. "As our—the Empire's—scouts probed deeper into the galaxy, they encountered the remains of a once-great interstellar culture, the Trelanquawelakin. . . . Call them the Trel.

"The Trel's planets were lifeless, devoid even of microbes. In the watery tombs that had been the Trel's cities, the Empire found evidence of a cataclysmic war of extermination.

"Somehow breaching the very fabric of space and time, vast armadas of ships had surged into our universe from another dimension. Without attempting contact, they began to methodically slaughter the peaceful, whalelike Trel, the only interstellar race of that time.

"Recovering from their initial shock, the Trel rallied and in battle near Cygnus—F18789105 Red to you, Captain—they routed the invaders, expelling them from our universe and sealing the breach. The primordial energies unleashed in that conflict rendered many of the nearby stars forever dark, a condition noted millions of years later by the Terrans, who dubbed the region the Coalsack.

"It was a pyrrhic victory for the Trel. Greatly weakened, their numbers depleted, they fell easy prey to the drone biophage ships scattered in their wake by the retreating foe.

"Dying, the Trel left a full account of their struggle for any race that might succeed them. An account and a warning: the breach could be reopened in about five million years.

"The Trel believed their nameless killers' mastery of transdimensional travel included also the dimension of time. The Enemy need only jump forward to the seal's dissolution and come through again."

Harrison was intrigued, despite his mistrust. "But the energy required for a time jump must be huge."

"True. Considering the Trel's figures—a billion ships, the smallest the size of this satellite—a time jump would drain the Enemy's galaxy, leave it a dry husk of black holes."

"They'd have to win through or die," said D'Trelna. "They couldn't retreat this time."

"The Enemy may not actually die, as we understand the term, Captain. The Trel finally captured a small enemy scout ship, enmeshing it in a webbed damper field. The two crewmen were inorganic: artificially created, silicon-based life forms."

"Robots."

"At what point, Mr. Harrison, does a machine become human? Where lies the threshold?

"These were highly individuated life forms, that much was apparent from their appearance. Alas, when the Trel turned the damper off, their captives blew themselves up. Took some of the Trel with them.

"That's all we know of the Enemy. If those machines were the Enemy, of course, and not just its servants.

"My task, given me by the greatest social engineers in the Empire, was to prepare humanity to withstand that invasion. As part of my charge was Terra and its people, I was established here. But I've watched the remains of the Empire over the centuries. You degenerated into a selfish rabble, concerned only with your own bellies, no more than a small police force for protection and possessed of the grand delusion that the universe would leave you alone.

"Well, it took me a long time, but I finally crafted the perfect enemy for you: merciless, hostile, utterly alien.

"I thought for a while, after you found they couldn't be bought off, that the S'Cotar would send you the way of the Trel. I was wrong. You rallied, counterattacked, forged an alliance. You were magnificent, more than fulfilling my fondest hopes. Well done."

"Would you really have let your biofabs destroy us, POCSYM?" asked D'Trelna.

"Yes. Such were my orders, Captain. If you couldn't survive the S'Cotar, what chance would you have against the Enemy?"

"This is all hypothetical, POCSYM," said John. "You have no evidence that the Trel were right. How could you—"

"Your pardon, sir. The breach reopened about one hundred and fifty Terran years ago. Two years ago, before they were detected and destroyed with alarming ease, my pickets signaled the advance of a vast armada through the breach. An armada of the sort described by the Trel. Their vanguard should be upon your outposts, Captain, in less than a year."

"Why should we believe you, POCSYM?" challenged the K'Ronarin. "You're the one who's been the father of lies. Why shouldn't we just put an end to this now?"

"If by 'putting an end' you mean to me, Captain, it will take far more than the ships now in bombardment orbit overhead. Contrary to an old Terran fable, the moon is not made of green cheese. It's made of shipbuster missiles, fusion batteries and half a million S'Cotar warriors.

"Have no fear, though. I'm forbidden to harm you."

D'Trelna gave a short, bitter laugh. "You kill millions of my people, then blandly tell me you're forbidden to harm us! My God! What warped minds must have programmed you!"

"Not warped. Just ordinary men, like you, trying to do their duty as they perceived it. Men who made a far greater sacrifice for their ideals than either of you will ever make.

"Enough. Your actions have proved my mission a success. You represent an armed, unified, vigilant humanity, the goal of my creators. Captain, I acknowledge your authority and submit to your arrest. Further, as a symbol of my good faith and proof of my ultimate veracity, I'll now destroy the S'Cotar."

Langston's image vanished. *Treachery!* hissed the mind-whisper. Gaun-Sharick stood before them again, antennae swinging in agitation. *You promised us the galaxy if we would but defeat these soft things!*

"It seems they're not so soft, Gaun. As for the galaxy—it was never mine to give. You had to take it. Yet with all the advantages I granted you, you failed. You're now only a dangerous encumbrance.

"In the S'Cotar bodies your researchers dissected, Captain, did you find a small protein chip grafted to the brain?"

"Yes. We thought it had something to do with the telekinetic abilities. The chips dissolved when removed, though."

"They're installed at birth by my servos and govern the telekinetic and telepathic gifts. Those chips make everything possible, including the bit of theater we've been enjoying: the battle on Terra, the wiping out of the biofab fleet.

"As Gaun-Sharick knows, the chips contain a matter/antimatter power source. And, as he also knows, they are my control over the S'Cotar. When they're outsystem, my drone ships pace them, armed with the kill code, ready to bring those dichotomous elements together.

"Most of the biofabs are now insystem, my effective range.

I'll now kill them. Stand clear of Gaun-Sharick. This will be messy."

Langston reappeared, eyebrow raised. Its smile broadened as the seconds passed. "Problem, POCSYM?"

"Captain," said POCSYM urgently, "the biofabs have immobilized my destruct programming and transporter capability."

In a fluid movement of arm and wrist, John drew and fired. The S'Cotar vanished an instant before it would have died. Harrison cursed softly, warily shifting his gaze about the catwalk.

"You must retake my control facility, Captain."

"Why? What have you done for us, POCSYM?" asked the Captain, unmoved.

"You can kill most of the biofabs, Captain. But it will cost you. You'll have to blow them out of the asteroids and moons, fighting against excellent defenses. I doubt, though, if you can take this base—not without extinguishing all life on Terra. This is a Class One Imperial Citadel. The S'Cotar can sit here and blast your fleet to pieces. Only a planetbuster could take this installation out.

"A ground assault is your only hope. With my help, it will work. I've already sealed off a direct route from a surface entrance to Central Control. Restore my destruct capability and this war is over. Also, only I know the location of a Trel stasis cache. You haven't a chance against the Enemy without it."

"Not much choice, is there?" said John.

D'Trelna shook his head. "No. All right, POCSYM. But first transmit the location of this alleged cache to my XO. If it proves a hoax, I'll personally take you apart with a spanner wrench."

"Complying now."

After confirming L'Wrona's receipt of a series of star coordinates, D'Trelna sketched the situation for Admiral L'Guan.

"You've lost your mind, D'Trelna!" exclaimed the senior officer. "An unknown base swarming with enemy troops—our men would be slaughtered, warsuits or not."

"Admiral, it's our only chance," replied the Captain with equal force. "This installation can stand up to a full fleet

bombardment forever. POCSYM's temporarily cut biofab reinforcements off from the control area. We must act now,
though.''

''Admiral, this is POCSYM. I can give your commandos
protection from most ground fire and get them through the
shield. But you must seize the moment. The S'Cotar will soon
break into the access route.''

There was a long pause on the comment, then a sigh. ''So be
it. I'll dispatch the entire brigade. God help us all, D'Trelna,''
L'Guan added fervently, ''if those boys walk into a trap.''

''Thank you, sir.''

''You've no transporter capability?''

''No.''

''Very well. You'll have to come out with commandos.
Rendezvous with them at POCSYM's Central Control. Good
luck.''

D'Trelna pulled his blaster. ''We're going to need more than
luck,'' he said, smiling lopsidedly at John. ''POCSYM, show
us the way to your control facility.''

CHAPTER 21

L'GUAN TURNED TO Captain S'Nar. "Signal Commander L'Wrona 'Away All Boats,' please, Captain. And stand by gunnery crews." His outer calm was in sharp contrast to his feelings. L'Guan hated sending men off to their deaths.

For political expediency, he was an Imperial—"Restore the Empire, restore our strength!" Secretly he loathed the movement and its leaders: jowly councilors, fascistic brother officers, unctuous politicos.

The Admiral had become a soldier because he was poor, and the only way up for a poor boy with smarts had been the Fleet. He'd worked hard, done well and risen slowly; they all had risen slowly till the S'Cotar came. When the war started, he'd been a commander with five ships that should have been scrap centuries before. Carefully hoarding his resources, L'Guan had distinguished himself in those first days by fighting sparingly, retreating slowly and buying time. Others—classmates, many—had died gallantly, throwing their lives away in suicide runs on the vastly superior S'Cotar fleets. Some few had broken and run.

One thing had led to another and now here he was, sending a lot of hard-nosed kids off to die because it really was the only way to win, to finally end it and take his men home. Most of his men.

L'Wrona received the attack order aboard one of the fifty assault boats orbiting between the fleet and lunar surface. "Take her in," he ordered the pilot. The stubby little craft banked, dropping toward the moon's dark side. Forty nine other boats followed in W formation. After five thousand years the Imperial Guard, led by its hereditary Lord-Captain, was going into battle again. As the engines whined higher, L'Wrona recalled his briefing by the Admiral.

"So that's it, Commander. I'm risking the entire Commando to end this war. You're clear on your orders?" L'Guan's image filled *Implacable*'s bridge screen.

"Yes, sir. Leading the Fleet Commando, I'm to assault a Class One Imperial Citadel, fight my way down two miles to POCSYM's Central Control area and secure it. I'm then to quickly repair any damage done to vital systems by S'Cotar sabotage and activate the biofab destruct sequence, thus killing the S'Cotar and winning the war.

"Also," he continued in the same sardonic tone, "should anything go wrong—how could it, though?—there are no reserves to save us.

"Lastly, no one has mentioned our returning."

"At least you have no illusions, Commander My-Lord-Captain," said the Admiral with a humorless grin. "POCSYM will get you through the shield, keeping it open for us to give you some surface cover. After that you're on your own. I'm sending over a briefing scan, furnished by POCSYM. It shows the way to his area, defenses, probable ambush points. It's very thorough."

"Thank you, Admiral."

"I knew your father, the late Margrave," continued L'Guan after a moment's hesitation. "We served together as ensigns— God!—thirty years ago, during the A'Rem 'police action.'"

L'Wrona nodded, a melancholy smile tugging at his lips. "He spoke of you often, sir. And of his days on the old *Steadfast* under Captain B'Tul."

"What a tub she was, L'Wrona!" He smiled broadly, old memories briefly wiping away his worries. "Worst destroyer in a fleet of derelicts. And B'Tul, that old martinet! Your father and I once let a F'Norian stinkbird loose in his cabin. What an uproar! Had us at battlestations for two days." His smile faded.

"I was grieved when I heard of his death, Commander," he added simply, the old hurt in his eyes not visible in the screen.

"He died well, sir," said L'Wrona with quiet pride. "Leading the counterattack on a S'Cotar bridgehead. He was cut down from behind by transmutes appearing as Planetary Guardsmen."

"That was a black day for all of us. You held the U'Tria port, I recall, long enough for survivors to escape."

"They didn't clear the atmosphere, Admiral. Enemy interceptors were everywhere." The younger man's face was expressionless.

"May we all do better today. The command is yours, Commander My-Lord-Captain L'Wrona," L'Guan said formally, saluting. "Bring them hell."

A sharp jolt broke the Commander's reverie. "Ground defenses have opened up," The pilot's voice sounded thinly over the commnet.

"It would have been better if you'd stayed behind," said L'Wrona, turning to the three figures strapped next to him in the boat's crash webbing. The rest of the boat's contingent were similarly suspended, a nest of warsuited spiders. The assault boats had no room for such frills as gravity generators or g-chairs.

"John's down there," said Zahava, tightening a strap. "But I do agree that Bill and André shouldn't be here—they're too old."

"I'm not too old," Sutherland said, his glare filtered out by the helmet's tint. "I jog two miles every morning. Besides, if I live through this, I can go on the lecture circuit, write my own ticket." Another sharp jolt interrupted him, swinging the passengers in their webs. "If I live through this," he repeated less certainly.

"I admit I'm too old," said Bakunin, hanging next to Sutherland. "I should be in my modest office at Three Dhzershinsky Square—it has a view of the Lubyanka—reading reports and ogling my secretary's legs."

"Then why the hell are you here?" Sutherland asked peevishly, the boat's evasive maneuvers beginning to affect his stomach. "The Order of Lenin?"

"The order of Comrade General Branovsky, Bill. Recall

that we're the only Terrans allowed aboard the Fleet, pending a formal exchange of ambassadors. . . .''

Sutherland gave a derisive snort. "The secret selection squabble at the UN could go on forever. Maybe we should ask POCSYM to build us a Terran ambassador acceptable to all Terrans!

"I'm sorry. You were saying?"

"That I'm here both to show the hammer-and-sickle and to keep an eye on you. The head of my Directorate told me, explicitly, what would become of me if you, capitalist lackey, went without me anywhere in the Fleet. The General's a Stalinist with a gift for vivid imagery. Thus we've toured a score of ships together and are now embarked on this pleasant excursion.''

Another near hit shook the boat.

"Missile," noted L'Wrona, calmly checking his blaster.

"Two minutes to target, Commander," the pilot called. "We're through the shield. I have the landing zone in sight."

"Attention, all boats," said L'Wrona. "Two minutes to target. Subcommanders, get your sections in position on the double. We've got to follow through on Fleet's salvo, overcome any outside resistance and enter the citadel before the enemy rallies.

"Good luck.

"And you three," he added to the Terrans, "stay close to me.''

Deep within the citadel lay Defense Control, nestled behind ten-foot walls of battlesteel, accessible only by teleport or transport. Tier upon tier of consoles filled the bowl-shaped room, screens flickering above them.

Gaun-Sharick arrived, answering an urgent summons.

They appear to be enemy scout craft, Glorious, reported the Watch Leader, antennae wavering uncertainly. *But that formation is unknown to us.*

Commando attack craft, replied Gaun-Sharick, watching a telltale. *The ion emission patterns are the same. And that's an Imperial assault formation. Note the double prongs. Idiots.*

Sound the alert. Reinforce our warriors in POCSYM's area. Signal all batteries to open fire.

The alarm went out, orders and responses flashing back and forth. Unwelcomed responses.

Impedance on all command-control circuits, Glorious. We cannot fire.

POCSYM. It was a dry curse. *Shield status?*

Maximum.

Start recircuiting missile batteries nearest Sector Red Twelve. They'll be trying for POCSYM's area.

New orders were issued. Nearer the surface, in hardened defense clusters, technicians began the laborious task of recalibrating scores of shipbuster batteries.

Have no concern, Glorious. The shield will stop them. If they tarry too long before retreating, we will have enough firepower to destroy them.

Perhaps. Carry on, Watch Leader. I'm going to Barracks Cluster Blue Thirty to oversee the reinforcing of Red Twelve.

Nothing happened. Gaun-Sharick remained where he was, unmoving. Then his thoughts came to every S'Cotar in the citadel.

Do not be alarmed. Some of our special ability is temporarily blocked. We of Command will soon remove the impediment.

Swarm Leaders, Blue Thirty, move your forces into Red Twelve. Use the old tube system. A human assault force is trying to reach POCSYM's Central Control. Kill them.

Surface Guard, Red Twelve, deploy.

Missiles firing in Red Twelve, Glorious. The Watch Leader's tentacles flew over his console. *Counterjamming now. Telekinesis will be restored soon.*

On thousands of channels, in ever-changing codes, creator and created fought.

The boats landed close to each other, churning up the dust in the small lunar valley. The webbing automatically retracted, the bulkheads dropping away. All but engines and pilot modules lay open to the vacuum.

"Deploy," barked L'Wrona, leading the rush to the nearest cover. In three minutes the one thousand men of his command were in position, a long, thin line of silver-suited figures extending along the base of a ridge.

L'Wrona signaled the advance. Reaching the ridge's crest in a series of practiced, graceful leaps, the troopers threw themselves prone in the ancient dust. Awkward, bounding at first in every direction, the three Terrans eventually reached the top, their bodies still uncertain in the light lunar gravity.

Below the humans lay a large box canyon. Suited figures with too many limbs moved from the far end, emerging from an entrance in the farthest wall. As the humans watched, more warriors poured into the canyon, leaping to take up positions on the flanking ridges—one of which now had human tenants.

"Hot time in the ol' town tonight," a voice murmured.

"Mr. Sutherland, your communicator's open," said L'Wrona. "Admiral, we're in position."

"Acknowledged," came L'Guan's voice. "Commencing fire."

Those who looked up saw a brilliant beam of red flash down from space. Stayed by an invisible hand, it halted a mile above the canyon. Hesitating briefly, the S'Cotar continued their advance, still unaware of the commandos.

More beams joined the first, forming a great cone of energy whose focal point began to glow—red, crimson, finally cherry. Too late the biofabs turned, scurrying back toward the gate.

In a soundless blast of showering rock, the fusion beams won through, becoming a hundred dancing spears that touched the S'Cotar surface guard, then vanished.

Nothing moved in the canyon.

L'Wrona stood, a lone silver man shining in silhouette against the rising Earth's soft pastels. Lying in the dust, Sutherland watched as the Commander raised the long-barreled blaster above his head. Despite his helmet's darkened glass, Bill had to squint against the fierce golden reflection from the inlay just below the weapon's safety: crossed swords beneath a five-pointed star, a device soft-burnished by the hands of the Margraves of U'Tria.

A young Daniel come to judgment, thought Sutherland even as L'Wrona cried, "Assault!" his voice long, wavering. It sounded to Bill more like an invocation than an order.

Gaining the canyon floor in a few long leaps, the humans

passed the S'Cotar's ashes, heading for the gate. At a hundred yards, L'Wrona halted his command with raised pistol. "Admiral, the gate, please."

A quick red lancet bored through the thick battlesteel, leaving behind a smoldering hole. Beyond stretched an empty corridor, most of its lighting still functioning.

A scream whirled the troopers about. Not all the biofabs had died in the bombardment. A hidden squad had sprung up, surprising the rear guard. Three men died before the massive return fire swept the warriors away.

L'Wrona turned back to the entrance. Blaster leveled, he warily entered the citadel.

There were no side corridors, the commandos found as they advanced; just the main one, leading to a very large elevator. "Ship lift," observed L'Wrona. "Too small for anything the S'Cotar have. Imperial Survey probably used it last. Let's see if it works." He pushed the call button.

The elevator arrived quickly, mammoth doors sliding noiselessly open. It was empty. The blasters raised to greet it slowly lowered.

"V'Arta," said the Commander, "remain here with your section to cover our withdrawal." His friend nodded, then began organizing the hundred men of C Section into a defense ring around the lift.

"H'Nar," said Zahava, laying a restraining hand on L'Wrona's shoulder, "how do you know the elevator isn't booby-trapped?"

"I don't," he said, stepping into the elevator. The first section trooped in past him. "I count on the S'Cotar's arrogance. They'd never have thought we could penetrate their home base. Time is short, Zahava. Coming?" The Terrans boarded.

The descent was rapid, uneventful, the levels flashing by on the big overhead indicator—levels marked not in S'Cotar, but in a large, unical script Zahava found she understood. "High K'Ronarin," L'Wrona explained. "The mother tongue of us all. K'Raoda thinks your own Indo-European root language one of its descendants."

"There are over two hundred levels so far!" exclaimed Bakunin.

"It was an Imperial Citadel, Colonel, not a granary," said the Commander.

"Positions," he ordered as the lift began to slow. "This should be POCSYM's level."

The commandos fell into three ranks—prone, kneeling, standing—and took careful aim as the elevator stopped. The shooting started even before the doors opened. Blue and red bolts sizzled past each other, tearing into the opposing ranks. Blasters whining, men screaming, biofabs hissing, the cloying stench of burnt flesh and everywhere the light: the beautiful killing light from the weapons, the rippling, rainbow aura of warsuits failing.

Bill had believed nothing could be as bad as that last battle under Goose Hill. He was wrong. This was an interminable moment of hell, a battle tableau from the art of Bosch or Floris.

L'Wrona brought them out of it, leading a charge into the biofabs, firing and clubbing with his pistol, stabbing with his knife. Short and vicious, the fight ended with the few surviving S'Cotar breaking for the safety of a cross-corridor. None made it.

"Without these warsuits, they'd be feasting on our corpses now," L'Wrona commented to Zahava as the humans regrouped and evacuated their wounded. The remainder of their force had now joined them.

"Do they really eat . . . us?" she asked, skeptical.

The K'Ronarin gazed for a moment at the heaped biofab remains, then led Zahava by the hand to one particular body. A well-aimed shot had ended the warrior's life, shattering its abdominal sack and deepening the viscous green slime covering the floor. Rolling the corpse over with his foot, L'Wrona pointed at a string of withered objects strung about the short neck. Zahava leaned closer, peering.

"Baby's feet!" she gasped, recoiling.

"Human infants are especially prized as a delicacy by the S'Cotar," said the officer, turning and walking away. "The necklace is a symbol of wealth and status. Maybe that was the commander of our reception party.

"Let's get moving before they counterattack.

"Section leaders, move your sections out on the double."

The golden, hovering sphere wavered twice before blinking out for good. D'Trelna spoke hopefully into his communicator. "POCSYM?"

". . . jam . . . cations . . . right . . . next . . ."

"Great. We've lost our guide," said John, looking down the long empty corridor. He counted fifteen cross-corridors in just the next half mile.

"D'Trelna to L'Wrona. Do you receive?"

Static filled the commnet.

"Jamming all right," grunted the Captain. "Sounded like POCSYM said 'next right.'"

The next right led down a narrow, curving corridor that ended at a door marked in the cursive S'Cotar script.

"Can you read that?" asked the Terran.

"'Spare Parts' . . . No." D'Trelna's brow wrinkled in concentration. "'Food Storage.' Maybe." He shook his head.

"Sorry I asked. Shall we take a look?"

John leading, they burst through the door. It was pitch-black inside. And cold. Very, very cold.

"Must be food storage," whispered the K'Ronarin. "Something wrong with the light activator? Ah!" he exclaimed as brilliant light flooded the room.

As long as he lived, John never forgot the shock of Greg Farnesworth's dead blue eyes staring into his own, inches away. His friend's naked corpse hung head down from the ceiling, wires through its feet running up to a simple block-and-tackle system. Dazedly, John stepped back, looking about the "storage" room.

Cindy's body—the Cindy Greg had never known—hung to the geologist's right. Behind them were Fred Langston's and over a hundred other corpses, all hanging like cattle in a slaughterhouse. Only Greg's cause of death was apparent: the hideous stomach wound from the *Nasqa* raid.

"Why?" John managed, finding his voice. His breath hung steaming in the frigid air. "Why take his body—anyone's body—and bring it here?"

Less shaken, D'Trelna noticed it first. "They've all been

brainstripped,'' he said with quiet horror. Now John saw it: the craniums had been neatly removed and the brains scooped out.

Harrison had survived much of war's meanness: Indochina with its napalmed children; nameless, massacred villages; pungi-staked GIs. He'd been with the South Africans when they'd raided across their border, an observer powerless in the face of infanticide, gang rape and throat slitting. John thought himself inured to man's bestiality. But this was a higher order of evil, an alien horror of unknown purpose. Choking back a throatful of bile, he turned to D'Trelna. ''Why brainstrip them? Why save the bodies?''

''First, how,'' said the Captain. ''POCSYM just transports the entire Institute staff here one quiet afternoon, instantly replacing them with S'Cotar transmutes. Like that.'' He snapped a blunt finger.

''How'd you know they were from the Institute, J'Quel?'' John asked softly. The K'Ronarin smiled to find himself staring down the wide bore of the Terran's blaster.

''You may just survive this war, my friend.'' He nodded approvingly.

''On the way here, you explained that the guise Gaun-Sharick took on the catwalk was that of the Leurre Institute's Director. When I saw the same face hanging from that meat hook over there, I drew the logical conclusion.

''Now''—he smiled—''would you mind pointing that blaster elsewhere? The M-Eleven-A has a notoriously delicate trigger, and your S'Cotar alarm is *not* signaling.''

''Sorry.'' Grinning sheepishly, he lowered the muzzle.

''Bah! You're just developing the right sort of reflexes.

''About the Institute, though, John. Why did POCSYM put a S'Cotar Nest on Terra? Any speculation?''

John stamped his feet, trying to warm them. ''I think he put it there so we Terrans would discover the S'Cotar. The events at the Institute and Goose Cove were as carefully orchestrated as the attack on your Confederation. It required less resources, but had to be timed with your arrival in this system.'' He paused. ''Could POCSYM have planted the clues in your Archives that led you here?''

''Possible. Archives is a vast, decentralized sprawl of a city, run by computers and a handful of academics. Yes, it's very possible.''

"But why brainstrip the corpses, J'Quel. What use could the S'Cotar have for human brains?''

They both saw it at the same instant. "POCSYM!''

"Of course!'' D'Trelna shouted, slamming his palm with a fist. "The S'Cotar didn't take them. *Revenge* wasn't the last mindslaver.''

"Damn right,'' growled John. "No wonder he's been able to keep going for all these centuries. His central components are infinitely renewable. And the corpses are saved—''

"As a treat for his creatures,'' finished the Captain. "Let's get out of here. My balls are frostbitten and I think I'm going to be sick.'' The officer turned toward the door.

"J'Quel, wait.'' Fanning the blaster wide, John fired into a stack of boxes. A second later the corpsicle room was filling with greasy smoke. Sullen orange flames began licking up the wall.

"*Requiescat in pace*, you poor bastards,'' said the Terran as the door slid shut behind them. He stopped dead. "But they really can't, can they?''

"Not while their minds are in thrall to POCSYM,'' D'Trelna said as they retraced their steps down the passageway.

"Then the only way to free them is to destroy POCSYM.'' John carefully scanned the intersection.

"Yes. And POCSYM will be destroyed, John, my word on it.

"Now what?'' asked the Captain, looking down the deserted corridor.

"Keep going in the direction we were headed when we lost contact with POCSYM. It stands to reason that the control area is off a main passageway. We know we're on the right level. So . . .'' He waved his blaster down the gray expanse of corridor.

"So we continue.'' D'Trelna sighed. "I'd travel easier in a warsuit.''

"Courage, Captain, courage,'' said John, slapping the older man on the back, some of his natural buoyancy recovered.

"Cunning and guile will win the day for us yet." He took off at a brisk trot.

"Let's hope Cunning and Guile get here soon," grumbled *Implacable*'s skipper, forcing his bulk after the other's slender, receding form.

L'Wrona picked himself up from the cold alloy of the passageway. Waving his pistol, he signaled the battered advance section to follow him through the carnage. He picked his way through the blasted corpses of the S'Cotar ambush force, mingled with the bodies of many—too many—of his men. Dropping back between the quick-trotting double file of commandos, he let his point squad take the lead.

"Feeling better?" he asked of a figure, slighter than most, keeping pace with the column. It was further distinguished by an ugly burn hole through its left arm.

"Yes, thank you, H'Nar," Zahava said drowsily. "The automedic's pumped me so full of painkillers I feel like I'm flying."

The attack, first since the lift, had been expected, even overdue. The length of time it had taken the biofabs to mount even minimal resistance to the assault had lent POCSYM some badly needed credibility. Perhaps the computer really *had* sealed the enemy from the humans' route of march. L'Wrona only hoped that D'Trelna and Harrison were finding it easy going to the rendezvous. The troopers' attack should have pulled every S'Cotar left in the sealed area into the counterattacks. But there'd been no contact with either the two men or Fleet since the commandos had penetrated the Citadel.

"The painkillers will wear off in a few hours, then all you'll want to do is sleep," said the Commander. "Sure you don't want to change your mind, go back to the boats with the rest of the wounded?"

"No way," the Israeli said firmly. "Although I don't think I'll take the point again."

She'd been leading the column when the biofabs hit from two side corridors. It had taken ten minutes of fierce hand-to-hand fighting before the ambush was overcome. The only survivor of the point squad, Zahava had led the final charge—this despite her wound.

"Still intact?" L'Wrona asked the two men protectively flanking Zahava. Like her own, their armor bore no rank, just the commando shoulder badge. Their winded condition was audible over the commnet.

"Physically, aren't we, André?" panted Sutherland.

"So far," the Russian grunted, blast rifle held ready at high-port, eyes suspiciously sweeping the side corridors as they trotted past. "I'd like more than that mendacious machine's word that these passageways are 'relatively secure.'"

"We've neither the time nor the force to secure them, gentlemen," said the starship officer. "All we can do is throw a squad down them as we approach, then pull it back after we pass. We can't get mired down in these labyrinthine halls. Everything depends on our reaching that control facility. Everything," he repeated grimly.

"Frankly," said Sutherland, hefting his rifle, "I preferred the reception aboard *Vigilant*. Give me canapés to carnage any day."

"You're a living symbol of capitalist decadence, Sutherland." Bakunin snorted contemptuously.

"You're hardly a paragon of socialist self-sacrifice, Colonel," retorted the CIA officer. "As we were changing into these warsuits, I noted your uniform. 'Chalmers of Savile Row.' Very nice."

"We all must make minor accommodations to the march of the dialectic," Bakunin said, unruffled.

It was then that the main counterattack materialized, literally, in the column's center.

Figures seemingly K'Ronarin, down to the last detail of insignia and equipment, appeared with blasters firing. Pandemonium threatened as the troopers tried to tell friend from foe in the ferocity of a head-on firefight.

The guard spheres saved them from the certain death of a rout. Their small, floating presence forgotten until now, they poured a steady, accurate fire into the transmute shock troops. Enjoying only the illusion of warsuits, the biofabs died. Seconds later the guard spheres self-destructed, settling to the floor in a sigh of melting circuitry.

"General assault from the side corridors!" crackled the commnet.

L'Wrona, with the Terrans, whirled to see a mass of biofab warriors overrun the squad holding the nearest intersection— an action being repeated the length of the column.

"Push them back! Do not pursue beyond the blast doors," ordered the Commander.

Rallying, the commandos sent a wall of flame into the bio-fabs, breaking their attack. Only at two points did the S'Cotar penetrate the column, breaches quickly scaled with biofab bodies.

Victory wasn't cheap, though.

Sutherland and Bakunin had joined a subsection attacking down a side corridor. The American, rifle empty, was laying into the warriors with his commando knife. Beside him, Bakunin flailed about with his rifle butt. The fighting was close, fierce and now in the humans' favor.

Suddenly the surviving biofabs broke for the safety of the next intersection. As they reached it, the great armored blast doors trundled shut in their faces.

"Nice guys!" Bill shouted to the Russian above the din. "'Stand or die!'"

The S'Cotar died—a desperate, hopeless charge. A few survived the blaster fire to throw themselves into the troopers' ranks. They, too, died. But not soon enough.

Sutherland had just slipped another chargepac into his rifle when the suicide wave hit. He shot the first few insectoids, then went down under three more. In seconds, Zahava and Bakunin had blasted the last S'Cotar from atop their friend.

"Let's go, Bill," Bakunin said, wearily extending a hand.

There was only a hoarse whisper in response. "Got me this time, André."

Only then did they see where the knife had torn a gaping hole in his stomach. Crimson blood flowed, mingling with the biofabs' green lifestuff.

"Hang on, we'll get you back to the boats," said Bakunin, removing Bill's helmet as Zahava called for a medic.

"Forget it," Bill whispered, face serene from the auto-medic's drugs. "Funny, isn't it, *Tovarich* Colonel? Think you've seen it all . . . spent final years pushing paper, then retire to—" A great cough racked his body. Blood dribbled from his mouth. ". . . cottage. What happens?" He smiled, more rictus than grin. "You end up fighting bug-eyed monsters with a KGB and some starship troopers." He coughed again, not as deeply.

Arriving with a medic and two stretcher-bearing commandos, L'Wrona overheard the last of Sutherland's eulogy. "You're not going to die!" he snapped. "You're going back with the wounded and into a medical regenerator. Then you're going to get well. Fast. Because there's a courier ship on the way with our new Ambassador. And the death of a Terran national under my protection would cast a definite pall over the treaty talks."

"You can't spare any more men to take out casualties," countered Bill weakly from the stretcher.

"I don't care if I have to storm that control area alone," L'Wrona snapped, eyes smoldering. "We always take out our wounded.

"Take him away. Safe trip."

Sutherland waved limply as his bearers joined a long line of similarly burdened soldiers. Zahava, L'Wrona and Bakunin watched as they disappeared around the corridor.

"Nor do we leave our dead for carrion eaters," said the Commander. "Give me a hand. You know what to do."

They'd watched before, after the other battles, as the troopers had set their dead comrades' weapons to delayed-destruct, placing them beneath the crossed arms of the fallen. This time they helped. It didn't take long.

"Move out!" L'Wrona ordered.

As his men double-timed by, he stood alone, saluting his dead for a long moment before joining the column.

The small, shrill explosions and pure white light raced toward the enemy, a sense of benediction in their wake.

CHAPTER 22

ONLY ONCE HAD Harrison and D'Trelna encountered biofabs: two sentries, head-shot before they could raise an alarm.

Cautiously peering around yet another curve in the seemingly endless corridor, the two men spotted a small group of biofabs busily erecting a barricade before a set of opened blast doors. The barricade faced the other way. The S'Cotar's backs were to them.

"D'Trelna to POCSYM," whispered the Captain for the hundredth time.

"Sorry for the inconvenience, Captain." POCSYM's voice was as assured as ever. "I've finally circumvented the biofabs' commbloc. You are at the control facility?"

"Yes. What's the status of the Fleet Commando?"

"They're twenty minutes from you, Captain, and coming fast. They have taken heavy casualties. I'm in contact with Commander L'Wrona."

"Can you put us in touch with them?" asked John.

There was a pause, a brief hum, then, "Captain, are you all right?" asked L'Wrona, concern in his voice.

"We're fine. What about you? POCSYM says you've sustained heavy casualties."

L'Wrona quickly sketched the raid's progress.

"There are just a few biofabs at the control facility," reported D'Trelna. "Why is that, POCSYM?"

"Many of this garrison went to man the ships you annihilated, Captain. The rest are busy trying to destroy your commandos or on their way to aid that effort. This is a large installation, though, so you still have a brief period of grace before Gaun-Sharick marshals his forces.''

"It's hardly been a cotillion so far," said L'Wrona.

"They've overcome all my attempts to block their route of march, Commander. But I still control most missile and beam defenses. And I've put a crimp in their teleportation. Reinforcements are approaching by traveltube.

"Fail at the control area, though, and you'll have a much warmer reception on the way back.''

"L'Wrona, this is John Harrison. I think the Captain and I can take that control room. Do you agree, I'Quel?''

The officer nodded. "I've been saving something special for just such an occasion.'' He tossed John a small black ball. "Stun grenade. Push the little button on the top, then throw. Detonates on contact.

"We'll take that control room, H'Nar, and hold it till you arrive. Ready?''

The Terran nodded.

"Toss on three. One. Two. Three.''

They chucked their grenades, then hugged the wall. As the teeth-rattling blast ended, the men charged around the corner. Blasting the stunned warriors, they dived between the closing doors.

The room was half the size of *Implacable*'s bridge. John counted twelve consoles, screens and equipment banks. Hearing a noise to his left, he ducked just as a bolt of raw, blue energy flashed by, blasting into the rear wall.

Rolling for cover, the men came up firing at the third console, blowing it apart in an explosion of flame and sparks. A S'Cotar ran crookedly from behind it, exoskeleton aflame. D'Trelna killed it with a negligent flip of his wrist.

"That's it,'' said John a moment later, after they'd carefully checked the room.

"Yes, but the door's broken,'' the K'Ronarin observed, pointing at the entrance. The blast doors stood a yard apart, unmoving. "I'll patrol the corridor. See if you can get POC-SYM's damage fixed.'' Easing his ample form through the narrow opening, the Captain vanished.

"Okay, POCSYM," John said to the air, "it's your show. What now?"

"It's always been my show, Mr. Harrison. It still is.

"On the fifth console to your right, there's a large red button labeled 'Fire Extinguisher.' It's the manual override. Please push it."

Holstering his blaster, John walked the few paces to the console, found the button and pushed. "Well?" he asked.

There was a brief silence. "Alas! They're very much alive, including the company now advancing down the corridor. I have alerted Captain D'Trelna."

"Sorry, POCSYM," John said wearily, walking to the door. "But I've no faith left in you *deus ex machina* types."

"J'Quel!" he called, stepping into the hall. "POCSYM says more biofabs are coming."

"I know." The Captain had settled behind the half-finished barricade. "He told me. How are you doing?"

"There are problems."

"Now what?" he asked, slipping back into the control room.

"Open the inspection hatch by turning the two fasteners at the upper corners clockwise.

"Now drop the panel and stand aside so I can see."

As he waited, John noticed two things: the machine's inside, evidently once a delicate, crystalline web, was now a fused blob. And the whine of blasters was coming from outside.

"I was afraid of that." POCSYM sighed.

D'Trelna backed hastily through the doorway, firing as he came. Blue bolts shot in after him, gouging chunks out of the wall. Some of the equipment began to burn.

Ignoring the destruction behind them, the two men knelt to either side of the opening, sweeping the passageway with a deadly crossfire. There was a sudden lull in the attack. D'Trelna risked a quick look.

"Not much cover behind that barricade," he observed. "They're falling back to regroup."

They both looked down, checking their weapons.

"So, what are you going to do after the war, John?" asked D'Trelna, slipping a fresh clip into his blaster. "At the risk of sounding banal."

"At the risk of sounding banal, J'Quel," Harrison said with a slight smile, eyes on the corridor, "I don't know. Before my friends and I stumbled into all this"—his free hand circled above his head—"I was going with the woman I love to a tiny country surrounded by enemies. Build a new life, raise a family, make a stand for a few simple verities."

"Ah, yes. The simple verities." The Captain nodded, smiling gently. "It's been a long time since I've seen some of them. Good friends, a shared life, peace in the land, joy in the children. Those sorts of things?"

"Yes." He glanced at D'Trelna. "Those sorts of things. But now . . ."

"But now you don't know."

"No. Oh, I still love Zahava. But this war—assuming we win—will open the galaxy to us, to Terra. Just the realization of that may well sweep away many of the underpinnings of my life—of several billion lives. In a decade I suspect that much of the political and cultural reality I've known will be supplanted by . . . what? You've brought us a large question mark, my Captain," he concluded quietly. "And what about you, J'Quel. Is your future as ambiguous?"

The Captain shook his head. "More settled, perhaps. I've got some back pay, savings, a modest pension and a brother-in-law who needs help running a cargo line. The guilds are eating him alive."

"I didn't know you had a sister."

"I don't."

"You're married—I mean, you have marriage?"

"Yes, I'm married." D'Trelna smiled. "And we do have marriage customs. Most of the societies in the Zone—I'm S'Htarian—practice polygamy. I'm away too much for that so R'Enna and I have a monogamous contract. K'Ronar Sector is strictly monogamous. As with much else, you might look to them for the origins of your mostly monogamous world."

He glanced down the corridor. "Here they come."

Raising their pistols, the men opened fire.

The return fire, closer than before, set more of the room on fire, filling it with an acrid, poisonous smoke. "They're working their way along the wall." D'Trelna coughed. "They'll toss a grenade in here soon."

"POCSYM, can't you do something about this smoke?" John managed to choke out.

"I have only observation functions left in this section. Sorry."

"Damned if I'm going to die of smoke inhalation. Let's take 'em." D'Trelna nodded.

Eyes streaming, they charged into the corridor, weapons ablaze.

L'Wrona rounded the bend at the head of the column just as D'Trelna and Harrison charged through the smoke, pouring a murderous fire into the S'Cotar. "Assault!" he shouted, firing even as the biofabs spotted the commandos.

The S'Cotar made a spirited stand. But though a match for the K'Ronarins in numbers, weapons and discipline, they had no warsuits. Their forward ranks blasted away by the troopers, their flank harried by the two men flitting in and out of the smoke, the warriors were soon compressed into a small, ragged square. A final volley of grenade and blaster fire finished them.

Gasping, their eyes bloodshot, D'Trelna and Harrison were given a boisterous reception by the attack force.

John was glad to trade the metallic air of the warsuit D'Nir brought him for the corridor's stench: burning machine and burnt flesh, both biofab and human. It'd been steadily tugging at his stomach.

A slight, wiry figure ran from the last subsection to arrive, throwing her arms around John, an embrace made cumbersome by rifle and helmet.

"You're all right?" they both asked at once, then burst into laughter.

"André and I are," the woman lied, trying to hide her arm. "But Bill's badly wounded. He's been medivaced to *Vigilant*."

"You *are* hurt!" Gently, John tugged Zahava's arm into sight from behind her back. "Why didn't you go back with the wounded?" he demanded angrily. "Ever the hero!"

"I'm a soldier!" the Israeli retorted, just as angry. "Don't think that just because you're a man . . . ."

A few yards away, another heated exchange was taking place.

"You're on a fool's errand, H'Nar," said D'Trelna, wearily pulling a warsuit on over his begrimed uniform. "POCSYM can't destroy the S'Cotar. The damage is too extensive. Once again, biofabs have bested their maker."

L'Wrona's joy at finding his friend alive was replaced by anger.

"I left a trail of ashes getting here, J'Quel. The ashes of good men—boys, most of them. And now you're telling me they died for *nothing*?!" He snapped the last word, glaring.

POCSYM's voice filled the air, ending the conversation. "The fault is mine. I underestimated the S'Cotar capacity for innovation and foresight. I have created a Frankenstein's monster, Mr. Harrison, Miss Tal, Colonel. A R'Actol Plague, Captain, Commander. Unlike those constructs' creators, though, I will accept the consequences of my actions.

"Reactors are now running to critical. You have ninety minutes to retrace your steps."

D'Trelna and L'Wrona exchanged alarmed looks. "Can we do it?" asked the Captain.

"Very little margin for error. Certainly not enough to live on, J'Quel." He managed a humorless smile, shrugging his shoulders. "Hell, we're not going to sit here praying.

"Prepare to move out! Section leaders, pick up your wounded. We're leaving on the double."

"POCSYM," John said as the troopers reassembled. "Are you a mindslaver?"

"Yes." The cool reply came over the tactical band. "I gather you found a cadaver room."

A cadaver room. "Yes. But you gave yourself away much earlier, when you first showed us *Revenge*. You laughed. K'Raoda told me that not even the Empire could program humor into its machines. Humor isn't logical."

"I'm afraid it was the young Subcommander's prattling about 'truth' that brought out the professor in me, Mr. Harrison. Several professors, actually." The ultimate mindslaver paused.

"But all of my original brainpods were filled by volunteers—dedicated men of vision who conceived this entire scenario. Men who truly had the courage of their convictions."

"No doubt they did," said John. "Fanaticism isn't a Terran

invention." The entire assault force was listening to their exchange, even as the men prepared to move out. "But how long did those original brains last? A thousand years? Surely no more.

"You're not just a Weapons system, as were the mindslaves aboard *Revenge*. You're a Planetary Operations Command System. Constant use would wear out many of your components, wouldn't it? Where did the replacements come from, POCSYM? Did you have the S'Cotar snatch Terrans? Did you later use K'Ronarin captives?

"How many through the centuries, POCSYM? Thousands? Hundreds of thousands?"

"A modest number, Mr. Harrison, when weighed against my mission: the preservation of humanity."

"A humanity you were prepared to sacrifice in order to save, POCSYM."

"My actions were necessary to ensure the survival—"

"Your actions were a five-thousand-year-old megalomania, inspired by men who believed themselves omniscient. Through you, they strove for omnipotence and immortality.

"You don't know if the human race, left to its own devices, wouldn't have stood off this alleged intergalactic menace. You merely assumed it wouldn't. And based on that assumption, you unleashed a horror upon your own people—a horror that almost destroyed them.

"Spare me your hollow piety, POCSYM. You're just an ancient malignancy left to fester in the body of galactic humanity."

L'Wrona led the column out, the wounded tucked into the formation's center. "Now we run the gauntlet," Bakunin commented, trotting behind John and Zahava.

It was one long, running battle. The biofab reinforcements had come up, filling every side corridor with warriors. Racing past each intersection, the humans were raked with blaster fire from hand weapons, shoulder arms and semis. Grenades rained down on them.

There was no time to clean out the S'Cotar ambushcades, not enough troopers left had there been time. Warsuit failures soared, casualties rose, suicide charges slowed the withdrawal.

The shrill of blasters self-destructing became a continuous, unnerving whine.

Gaun-Sharick stood before the Council of the Magnificent, the only five S'Cotar who equaled him in age and rank. Evacuation klaxons sounded from outside the chamber.

Can interplanet teleportation be restored? asked Tuan-Lagark, the Senior.

Not before POCSYM blows us up. There was a tinge of anxiety to Gaun-Sharick's thought.

Tuan-Lagark's antennae wove an acceptance-resolution pattern. *You are the last hope of our race, Gaun-Sharick. Allow the humans to escape. Go with them, biding your time till you can call forth our deep-hoarded strength.*

You can deceive their instruments? asked another Councilor.

Easily, Luan-Ortar. I march with their men, sleep with their women and they know me not. He touched the medallion about his throat. *Wearing this, I am safe.*

Go then. Revenge us and restore the Race.

He bowed low and was gone.

L'Wrona moved up and down the column, ordering, pleading, cajoling.

"Close up.

"Watch your flank, there.

"Section Leader U'Trna, send two squads to reinforce the rear guard.

"Sergeant, help that trooper, he's hit.

"That man's dead. Cycle his blaster.

"Come on! Come on! Pick up the pace!

"You're not tired. Commandos never tire."

It was the voice of POCSYM, though, that really kept them going, methodically counting the waning moments.

"Sixty minutes to destruct.

"Forty-five minutes to destruct."

At destruct minus twenty, singing mixed with the blasters' shrill.

"What's that?" L'Wrona demanded, not breaking stride. The gauntlet run, they were nearing the lift. The rear guard now bore the brunt of the counterattack.

"It's the Soldiers Chorus from the Terran opera *Aïda*, Commander, the tragic tale of two star-crossed lovers who die entombed together. You'll never know how singularly apt it is for my funeral."

The point squad reached the lift. "I'm in contact with G Section, Subcommander V'Arta," the squad leader—D'Nir—reported. "They're under heavy attack."

Jogging into sight of the lift, L'Wrona was finally able to raise V'Arta. "What's your status, N'Trol? Topside secure?"

The whine of massed energy weapons filled L'Wrona's ears as V'Arta reported.

"For now, H'Nar. But you'd better get up here fast. Most of us are dead."

"E and G Sections, into the lift," the Commander ordered. Pointing to three familiar figures, he added, "You stay here until we've secured ground level."

Harrison and Zahava supported a third, limping form between them. "I'm going with you, H'Nar," said John. "But would you detail someone to help Zahava with Colonel Bakunin? He tried to stop a suicide wave by himself." A burn hole gaped halfway up the Russian's right leg. Half the calf muscle was gone. "Anna?" he murmured, drowsy from the narcotics, as a burly sergeant took John's place.

"Ten minutes to destruct," said POCSYM as the elevator rose.

"I regret I can't dispose of all the biofabs for you," it continued. "You'll have to clean their remnants out of this system, especially the few left on Terra. And some of their ships are still loose in the galaxy. They'll menace shipping and isolated colonies for some years.

"I am now transmitting the locations and defense specs of all biofab secondary bases to your flagship, Commander."

The lift opened on C Section, dying in an ocean of biofabs.

"C Section, drop!"

The troopers fell away, leaving a clear field of fire.

"Shoot!"

To John, firing from the third and standing rank, their volley seemed a great river of red flame smothering the packed bodies fused into a charred wall around C Section's few survivors.

"Secure the area," ordered L'Wrona, sending the lift back down. "V'Arta?" he called, looking about.

"Dead," said a badly wounded corporal as a medic reached him.

"Seven minutes, Commander, max," warned POCSYM as the lift disgorged two more sections. "Stability's decreasing. It could actually go anytime."

L'Wrona seemed not to hear.

"*Vigilant* to ground force," came the Admiral's voice over the commnet. "Advise status."

L'Wrona said nothing. He stood unmoving, looking at the charnel house that had been C Section.

"Sir?" said a commtech, touching the Commander's arm.

L'Wrona shook his head. "Ground force," he said dully. "That you, D'Trelna?"

"No, sir, L'Wrona. The Captain joined us but insisted on commanding the rear guard. He should be here at ground level in a few moments. Sir," he continued, some vitality coming back into his voice, "it's imperative that the boats be brought into the canyon adjacent to the Citadel entrance. We—"

"There and waiting, Commander. POCSYM's been sharing the countdown with us. Get your command out of there."

The third and final load of troopers came off the lift, D'Trelna at their head. "I heard that," he said. "Come on, H'Nar, let's get the wounded and run! We've got—"

"Five minutes to destruct," POCSYM intoned.

"To the boats!" shouted L'Wrona, waving toward the blasted gate.

John ran for his life, staggering under the weight of the half-dead commando over his shoulder, lungs bursting, pain shooting up his legs. With agonizing slowness, the black circle that was the tunnel's end grew larger, framing the heads of those in front of him. The black of space drew him, moving him on despite the searing pain filling his chest. The black was freedom: freedom from the Citadel's G-generators, from the S'Cotar, from the ancient evil that was POCSYM. Freedom, for a while, from death.

A red haze of exhaustion blurring his vision, John broached

the surface, breaking free with a single, soaring leap and bounding toward the boats.

"Go! Go! Go!" shouted D'Trelna, as what was left of the raiders scrambled into the landing craft.

They were fifty miles up and banking sharply when a hole miles wide was punched through the lunar rock, sending dust, atomized metal and S'Cotar into space.

Orderly chaos ruled *Vigilant*'s Hangar Deck. Crash crews and fireguards raced to the boats, ready if the explosion had torn up the craft. Medics in hovering medcarts rushed in behind them, quickly moving out the wounded.

High on the glass-walled hangar bridge, K'Raoda and one of *Vigilant*'s subcommanders watched a set of telltales, prepared to seal the Hangar Deck, wounded or no, if a S'Cotar trace showed.

With all boats in and the scan negative, they went down to help.

L'Guan and McShane found L'Wrona, D'Trelna and the Terrans sitting hollow-eyed on the deck, drained, their gear scattered around them.

L'Guan started to speak, then stopped. Turning to his aide, resplendent in braided dress uniform, he said tersely, "Anything they want, get it." Slowly he walked away, the spring gone from his step.

No one seemed to notice as Bob bent over, kissed John and Zahava, then left without a word, following the long line of medcarts into the heart of the ship.

CHAPTER 23

PRESIDENT MARTIN HAD appeared on prime-time TV a week after the lunar battle, an address preceded by the wildest spec ulation; speculation fueled by rumors of clandestine military operations along the New England coast. Rumors that President MacDonald and CIA Director Tuckman hadn't been killed when Air Force One crashed into the sea. Rumors of a secret Red Alert called at a time of abnormal international calm. And rumors of strange radar reports, leaking through the suddenly tightened security nets of a dozen nations.

Martin's delivery of the facts about POCSYM, the K'Ronarins and the Biofab War was made in his usual crisp, dry Iowan tone; he might have been lecturing on torts.

The pampered Washington press corps, already inconvenienced by the President's choice of the Capitol's West Portico for his news conference, were further miffed by the difficulty in getting there: the Mall and all adjacent streets had been closed without explanation, creating an unmoving Friday evening gridlock. Many of the reporters had to trot the final mile from their stalled, overheated cars.

Tired, sweaty, at first they weren't sure what they were hearing. By the time Martin had finished, though, everyone knew he'd cracked, latest victim to the pressures of high office.

"Poor s.o.b.," whispered the *New York Times* to Reuters in the embarrassed silence following the statement. Reuters said nothing, instead turning the *New York Times* around with a hand to her shoulder, pointing at the great bulk of *Vigilant* as she came in over the Tidal Basin, blotting out the night sky.

Silently hovering over the Mall, she filled it from Monument to Capitol, every instrument pod, weapons blister and observation bubble a blaze of light.

It was the biggest party Earth had ever seen. Wherever the K'Ronarin landed—and they landed only by invitation—the formal reception quickly became a street festival lasting days. When it finally ended and the guests had gone back to their ships, life went on much as before. But with the expectation that things would soon be changing.

They would.

The hundreds of Treaty signators pledged their nations' help against the presumptive Enemy. The K'Ronarins, in return, promised technical aid, colonization rights throughout the galaxy and the option of Terran application for Confederation membership. This last would bring with it the stardrive, the catch being that application had to be a unanimous one from all sovereign Earth states. And there was still one holdout.

The fat old man stood at his window, watching an angry red sunrise fire the gold capping Ivan the Great's bell towers. The East is Red. He snorted, turning back to his desk with its heap of reports detailing the dissolution of the Warsaw Bloc, the ongoing disintegration of the Soviet Empire.

Sighing, he poured himself another shot of vodka, tossing it down with practiced indifference. Leaning back in the creaky old armchair, big feet on the desk, he unbuttoned his shirt collar. Heavy with medals and ribbons, his uniform jacket lay in a crumpled heap on the ancient horsehair sofa. Lacing his fingers over his impressive gut, the old man again counted the cracks in the high white ceiling, ignoring the polite knock on his door.

At the second, less tentative knock, he grunted, "Come.

"Ah, Bakunin." He sat up, taking in without comment the other's battledress and assault rifle, then poured himself another shot. "Care for a drink, Andreyev Ivanovich? Or should I call you André, as your Western friends do?"

Silent and grim, Bakunin shook his head, then cleared his throat. "Sir, I have the unpleasant duty of placing you—" he began formally.

The old man waved the bottle at him. "Please, André, why the haste? You New Decembrists have always been a slow and careful group. Why not savor your victory?"

Bakunin couldn't hide his surprise. "You knew?"

"Of course we knew." He took another shot, finishing the bottle. "Not enough and too late. But we knew. Don't forget, we played this game a long time." The nearby chatter of automatic weapons briefly turned their heads.

"I was seven when Lenin and Trotsky took the Winter Palace, André. Never thought I'd outlive the Revolution." More intense, the gunfire drew nearer.

"Perhaps, sir, the Revolution has outlived itself," said Bakunin with a wisp of a smile.

The head of KGB's Second Chief Directorate gathered himself in, sitting up at his desk. "I'd be interested in your analysis of how we came to this moment, and the part your most recent assignment had in it. Did the Biofab War do this to us?" His hand swept over the reports.

Bakunin shifted his weight uneasily. "It served as a catalyst for much that would eventually have happened.

"The Presidium's refusal to ratify the Treaty cut us off from K'Ronarin technical aid. We'd have been thrown back three hundred years, the primitives of Europe—of the world this time."

Z'Sha, the courtly K'Ronarin Ambassador, had taken the UN Security Council veto graciously, going on to sign separate treaties with every member nation of the General Assembly save one.

"All it took was a spark, once the word got out. Poland flared up over food—nothing new. In a week, though, Hungary, East Germany and Czechoslovakia had risen, Yugoslavia had seceded. We were in the midst of the Third Revolution. In two weeks, Georgia led the Autonomous Republics in revolt. All the armies in the world couldn't have stopped it. Ours mostly disintegrated, caught by a tidal wave on the floodplain of history."

"And had we ratified the Treaty, André? Would that have saved us?"

"Ratifying the Treaty would only have postponed it, sir.

Not ratifying it compressed fifty years of social evolution into a single month.''

The gunfire stopped abruptly. "Get it over with, Colonel. You're a Russian officer. Do your duty.''

Bakunin all but came to attention, thumbs at his pantseams. "Colonel General Mikhail Ilarionovich Branovsky, I arrest you in the peoples' name.

"I urge you, sir, to advise those KGB units still holding out that further resistance is futile. The army, air force and Strategic Rocket Force are with us.''

Branovsky nodded absently, walking slowly back to the window. He stood, hands clasped behind his back, staring down at the small riot of color in the gray-cobbled courtyard. "Take good care of my tulips, André. They're more delicate a perennial than you'd suspect.''

Going to the sofa, he put on his jacket and buttoned it, smoothing it with his big peasant hands.

"Shall we go?" he asked, taking his cap from the coat rack. "I gather the Motherland requires one last service of me.''

"I don't believe it.'' With exaggerated care, John dazedly set the phone back on the patio table.

Zahava looked up from her coffee, concerned.

"That was our agent,'' he said slowly. "The book . . .''

"They didn't turn it down!'' she cried.

Returning from *Vigilant*, John, Zahava and Bob had worked day and night for three months on their book, *First Contact*. It was all there, from their first meeting with Bill to the final battle. John had air-expressed it off to New York last Friday and never been far from the phone since.

Before he could reply, McShane, Bill Sutherland and a third man came out onto the patio from the townhouse.

"Look who dropped in!'' boomed McShane.

"André!'' They rose to greet the Russian.

"In the flesh.'' Bakunin grinned, sinking into a chair. But for the close-cropped hair he might have been an assistant professor, with his corduroy jacket, leather-patched at the elbows, casual summer pants and penny loafers.

"Nice house.'' He nodded approvingly. "At heart I'm a reactionary: the older I am, the more I like fine old things.''

Climbing just above the brick wall, the hot August sun had coaxed open the last of the morning glories. A pair of cardinals flirted in the big old elm overhanging the wall, red and gray plumages soaring high into the greenery.

"So, what brings you to the States, André?" asked John. "A well-earned rest?" Ex-CIA, it was the closest he could come to open admiration for the ex-KGB.

The dramatic footage of Bakunin helping a pale, stumbling Raoul Wallenberg through the Lubyanka's shattered gate had swept the globe. Imprisoned most of his life by a system unable to admit error, the elderly Swedish diplomat, a hero of the Holocaust, looked thin but well. He'd even made a brief but gracious speech before boarding the 727 that took him home to Stockholm and a jubilant welcome.

"K'Ronarin liaison." The Russian sipped a cup of coffee. "I'm going on the Trel Expedition. But first I have one small chore to perform at the K'Ronarin mission office in New York. And besides"—he smiled—"I wanted to tour the world's greatest tourist attraction."

"So you're going out to Andrews to tour *Vigilant*?" Bob asked. Bakunin nodded, crossing his legs. "I'd think you'd have seen enough of her."

"Oh, I have. But I want to see her here on Earth, with crowds lined up outside her. Then maybe I can accept that this has all actually happened. Call it a pilgrimage for my psyche's sake." He unconsciously rubbed his healed calf muscle.

"Then?" asked John.

"Then to New York. I'm empowered by my government to sign the Terran/K'Ronarin Treaty."

"Thank God." McShane sighed, standing to shake the surprised Colonel's hand. "And thank you, André. This hand I'm holding will free us from our small pocket of the universe."

"And how's the CIA's new Director?" asked Zahava, lighting a cigarette as Bakunin looked thoughtfully at his hand.

"You mean 'the dedicated Intelligence officer whose brilliance and daring saved not only his country but his planet'?" quoted John, smirking maliciously.

"No more, please," pleaded Bill, holding up his hands. "The President was too effusive—you've no idea how horrible it is to be anointed a demigod! People at work vying for the honor of bringing me coffee, Emmy-chan won't let me take out the trash. And I get swamped when we go out—too many people know my face." He shook his head. "No wonder you three wouldn't let the President or me mention your contributions."

"Otherwise?"

"Otherwise, Zahava, I'm busy, keeping track of the fledgling democracy in Russia, liaison with L'Guan and Z'Sha's people helping organize the Expedition."

Bob hesitated, then buttered another croissant. "When does that leave?"

"As soon as Fleet mops up the S'Cotar in our system. Maybe two months." Adding a generous glob of boysenberry jam to the roll, he took a heroic bite.

"D'Trelna's going to lead it," said Sutherland. "He's been promoted Commodore. And L'Wrona's now Captain of *Implacable*."

Reaching under the table, John brought the cold bottle of Dom Pérignon and some champagne flutes out from their hiding place. "I have two announcements." The loud pop of the cork scattered the cardinals.

"One." He began pouring. "Our book has been sold to a publishing consortium for an advance of five million dollars."

McShane choked on his croissant, then drained his glass in one gulp. Zahava's jaw dropped. Sutherland and Bakunin pounded backs and pumped hands, loudly congratulating the trio.

When the tumult died, John continued. "Two. Captain, Miss Tal and I are getting married next weekend by a compliant rabbi. You're all invited." Zahava's anguished "I don't have a dress!" was drowned by boisterous best wishes.

"And I also have an announcement," she said as Harrison refilled the glasses. "Admiral L'Guan's accepted John's and my application to join the Trel Expedition."

"What application?"

"The one I submitted last week through Bill."

John put down his glass. "Mindslaves. Matter transport. Biofabs. Machiavellian cyborgs. Hostile space. The 'Enemy.' And worst of all, gallant allies." He tossed down the wine. "I can hardly wait."

Bill reached over, touching his arm reassuringly. "Don't worry, John," he said solemnly. "I'll be with you."

"And you, Bob?" asked Zahava hopefully.

"Thank you, no," the philosopher said firmly, topping his glass. "I'm going to spend my dotage with the grandchildren.

"Besides," he added cheerfully, "one of us should stay and see to the spending of the royalties. But I'll think of you while I'm on Capri."

"My friends," said John, slightly tipsy, "my dear friends, a great writer once said mankind would not just endure, but prevail, so long as we realized always that the basest of all things was to be afraid.

"A final toast, then," he offered, golden glass held high.

"To humanity and its future, bright and unafraid!"

"To the future!"

MORE SCIENCE FICTION!

ADVENTURE